What kids are saying about
Cheesie Mack

"Hey, Cheesie!!! I am a BIG fan right after reading your book
a few minutes ago. You and Georgie are awesome!!!"
—Max, Singapore

"Your book was amazilicious! I ate it right up!"
—Lila, New York

"I read the whole book in two hours, it was so good."
—Hunter, Texas

"I totally love your book! P.S. I love mack and cheese too!"
—Amanda, Wisconsin

"I can't wait until your next book."
—Liam, Alberta, Canada

"I loved your book! I just finished it and as soon as I did,
I ran to my computer and went on your website."
—Cara, Connecticut

"This is the best book I've ever read!"
—Michael, Illinois

"Cheesie Mack is the best!"
—Monica, Massachusetts

"Ronald Mack, you have grabbed my
funny bone and tickled it!"
—Tanvi, South Carolina

"Keep writing, Cheesie Mack!!!"
—Ella, California

READ ALL OF CHEESIE'S ADVENTURES!

CHEESIE MACK
IS NOT EXACTLY FAMOUS

STEVE COTLER

Illustrated by Douglas Holgate

A YEARLING BOOK

Text copyright © 2014 by Stephen L. Cotler
Cover art and interior illustrations copyright © 2014 by Douglas Holgate

All rights reserved. Published in the United States by Yearling, an imprint of Random House Children's Books, a division of Random House LLC, a Penguin Random House Company, New York. Originally published in hardcover in the United States by Random House Children's Books, New York, in 2014.

Yearling and the jumping horse design are registered trademarks of Random House LLC.

Visit us on the Web! randomhouse.com/kids

Educators and librarians, for a variety of teaching tools, visit us at RHTeachersLibrarians.com

Visit Cheesie at CheesieMack.com!

The Library of Congress has cataloged the hardcover edition of this work as follows:
Cotler, Stephen L.
Cheesie Mack is not exactly famous / Steve Cotler ;
illustrations by Douglas Holgate. — 1st ed.
p. cm.
Summary: Cheesie and Georgie unearth an artifact from Colonial times and become middle school celebrities.
ISBN 978-0-385-36984-8 (trade) — ISBN 978-0-385-36985-5 (lib. bdg.) — ISBN 978-0-385-36986-2 (ebook)
[1. Antiquities—Fiction. 2. Celebrities—Fiction. 3. Best friends—Fiction. 4. Friendship—Fiction. 5. Family life—Massachusetts—Fiction. 6. Middle schools—Fiction. 7. Schools—Fiction. 8. Massachusetts—Fiction.] I. Holgate, Douglas, ill. II. Title.
PZ7.C82862Chh 2014 [Fic]—dc23 2013011798

ISBN 978-0-385-36987-9 (pbk.)

Printed in the United States of America
10 9 8 7 6 5 4 3 2 1
First Yearling Edition 2014

Random House Children's Books supports the First Amendment and celebrates the right to read.

For my parents, Edith and Ted.
Her unsung brilliance gave a small boy the
tools to sculpt a life. His arms-wide songs and
stories gave that boy the palette to paint it.

Contents

CHEESIE MACK
IS NOT EXACTLY FAMOUS

Chapter ∞

After ... The End

This book contains the complete story of my fourth adventure.

Is it all true?

Yes!

I should know. I wrote it. I'm Ronald Mack, but everyone calls me Cheesie. I'm a sixth grader at Robert Louis Stevenson Middle School in Gloucester, Massachusetts.

But this is not the beginning of my book. Even though most authors put the beginnings of their books at the beginnings of their books, I don't.

Right here, right now is actually the end of my story. You're reading what comes after chapter 21, which is at the back of this book, and if you looked at the table of contents it's called "Hello, Kitty!" (But if you think it's about a Japanese girly thing, forget it! You're wrong.)

So now I'm writing this chapter after I already wrote "The End," which is why this is called "After . . . The End."

And since my dad told me infinity is the end of numbers, and nothing comes after it, I named this chapter with an infinity sign. That's what the squiggle that looks like a sideways eight at the top of page 1 is.

Anyway, if you keep reading, you'll find yourself in my fourth adventure, which contains some very unusuweird* stuff:

1. 100-year-old pizza
2. super-sticky mud
3. Pocahontas
4. slime mice
5. osmium
6. stinking, rotting whale blubber

You'll also read about the continuing problems I

---

* I made up *unusuweird*. Do NOT use it in school writing . . . your teacher will not understand!

have with my older sister. When this book starts, the score of the Point Battle between me and her is 735–694. I am way ahead! You'll have to read all the way to chapter 21 to see what the score is now. (The rules are on my website.)

Mostly this adventure has to do with how I become sort of famous. It takes place in October and starts while I am asleep.

I hope you like it. If you do or you don't or you want to tell me something about this book or about yourself or what the kid who sits next to you in math is like, you can write to me on my website.

Signed:

Ronald "Cheesie" Mack

Ronald "Cheesie" Mack (age 11 years and 4 months)

CheesieMack.com

Chapter 1

Total Mud War

I am eleven years old. That's not very old, but there's one thing I know for sure. Every single moment of my life (and yours, too!) might be the beginning of a new adventure. You never know what's coming next. And mostly you never know an adventure has begun until you're already into it.

It was a Monday morning in mid-October.

"It's raining cats and dogs out there." That was the first thing I heard when I awoke. It was my dad, rumbling in the hall outside my bedroom. My head was still on my pillow, and my eyes were shut. I listened to the raindrops drumming on my roof.

Cats and dogs . . . , I thought.

I lay there wondering what it would sound like if cats and dogs were actually bouncing off my roof.

It would be way noisy. Probably meowingly and barkingly loud!

That thought woke me up more, because I asked myself, *Why do people say "cats and dogs"? Why not "cows and sheep"? Or "aardvarks and antelopes"?*

I know. You think I'm weird.

Well, you're right. I am. Sometimes I get wondering about something, and I just won't let go of it until I know what it's all about.

So I popped out of bed and flipped on my computer. I looked over at Deeb, my springer spaniel and the best dog in Gloucester. She hadn't moved from the foot of my bed, but her eyes were on me.

"I am looking up something about your species. Pay attention, mutt."

She didn't seem to care, and just closed her eyes.

A few minutes later, standing there in my pj's and sort of hopping from foot to foot because I had to pee, I found out that "raining cats and dogs" probably comes from long-ago England. If a rainstorm was really huge, the water would wash everything down the streets, including any dead pets and strays that had been tossed into the gutters.

Ugh. Gross.

Kind of made me appreciate the garbage trucks that come through our town every week.

I ran to the bathroom and returned just as my cell phone burped. (I recorded Granpa belching and turned it into a really cool ringtone that blorps "riddle-dee-diddle" whenever I get a text.)

It was from Georgie: Byx nix. Dad ya.

Georgie is much better at texting than I am. But sometimes it's hard to figure out what he means. This one, however, was easy. I looked out my window at the "cats and dogs" pouring down from the sky. His text meant we weren't going to ride our bikes (byx) to school. His father would drive us.

Granpa uses the word *nix* all the time. It means nothing.

I'm serious. It actually means nothing.

I mean *nix* means *something*, but the something it means is actually "nothing." Granpa told me it comes from the German word *nichts*, which is pronounced almost the same as *nix*. *Nichts* means "nothing" in German. Granpa was born in Germany. He came to America when he was five, so his first language was German. But he never talks about his childhood. I think it was bad or something.

I trotted downstairs for breakfast. My sister, Goon, had just put her dishes in the sink and was heading out the door. Mom had left for work hours ago. She's an air-traffic controller at Logan Airport in Boston. And Dad was already out somewhere driving somebody around in one of the limousines he owns.

Granpa cracked an egg for my breakfast into a frying pan. He stared into the pan, then looked at me with a squinty-evil-eye. "Hey, kiddo," he said. "How would you like it if I guaranteed you a day filled with nothing but good luck?"

"That would be fine," I replied cautiously. Granpa was up to something. The squinty-evil-eye was my clue. That's what we Mack guys do when we're pulling tricks or kidding around or something.

"Clap your hands three times."

I clapped.

He flipped my egg over. "Grab your left ear with your right hand, hop on your right foot, and spin around twice."

I grabbed, hopped, and spun.

"Now say the alphabet forward and backward, leaving out all the vowels."

I messed it up. (You can hear Granpa doing it on my website.)

"Doesn't matter, my young Mack boy," he said as he slid a single egg with two yolks onto a plate. "All that was just me goofing on you. Lookee this!"

Granpa pointed two fingers in a V at my egg. "A double-yolker! That means you are on the way to a very-very lucky-lucky day-day."

"Cool-cool." I grinned, gave Granpa a high-five, and sat down to eat.

(Later that day I looked up double-yolk eggs on a school computer. Some people believe a double-yolker is good luck. I don't really believe in any of that superstition stuff—omens or black cats or whatever—but if you read further, you'll see if Granpa was right.)

On the drive to school, it was raining so hard, Mr. Sinkoff's wipers couldn't sweep the water off the windshield fast enough, so he had to stick his head out the window and drive super slowly. But it was a warm October day—Indian summer is what we call that kind of autumn weather in New England—so even though he got drippingly wet, Mr. Sinkoff laughed about it.

At school, just as Georgie and I entered class, the room lit up with a flash of lightning.

Instantly Glenn Philips started counting out loud.

"One thousand one . . . one thousand two . . . one thousand three . . ." He had just passed seven when a huge clap of thunder surprised us.

A couple of kids shrieked. One dropped a book.

"That lightning is about one and a half miles away," Glenn announced calmly.

Georgie looked out at the dark sky. "How can you tell?" he asked.

"It takes sound just about five seconds to travel a mile," Glenn explained. "Light travels almost a million times faster. That's why we see the lightning flash almost instantly. But it takes a while for the sound to reach us. So, if you count the seconds from the flash until you hear the thunder and divide by five, the result is the number of miles away."

Glenn is the smartest sixth grader at our school. I'm convinced of it. If you want to see how he figured all this out, go to my website. I let him put up a page there to explain it. He also explains how you can tell what the temperature is by counting cricket chirps.

Just then there was another lightning flash. I started counting thousands along with Glenn. We both were up to nine when another BOOM shook the windows.

"That one was louder," Georgie said.

"But farther away," I said. "Almost two miles."

"That would suggest the storm is moving away from us," Glenn said.

He was right. There was lots more thunder and lightning, but a half hour later it stopped raining, the sun came out, and the rest of the day was same old, same old school. Some work, some fun. It was good, but absolutely nothing was the least bit unusual.

That's why I did not suspect the beginning of an adventure was just a few hours away.

My last class was physical education—we call it PE or phys ed. The all-night rain had left the fields super muddy, so we stayed inside and played volleyball in the gym. Afterward, most of the boys changed back into their regular clothes, but Georgie and I didn't. All I switched was my shoes, because I had cross-country practice (I'm second fastest on the sixth-grade team). And because Georgie had a basketball game starting in an hour, he put on his red and blue uniform. It has

RLS on the front and a big 11 on the back. His stenchy gym clothes were in a repulsive pile on the bench next to me.

"When are you going to wash those?" I asked.

"Never!" Georgie bragged. "I'm helping the environment by saving water."

"More like destroying the environment by polluting the atmosphere," I replied, holding my nose. Georgie reached out to grab me, but I dodged away and trotted toward the door. "I'll zoom through my practice run. I'll be there for the start of your game."

"Take your time. I won't be playing, remember?" Georgie held up the splint on his broken finger. (If you read my last book, *Cheesie Mack Is Running Like Crazy!,* you know about the Cheesie–Georgie backyard jousting match that caused it.)

"Who cares about you?" I kidded. "I want to see Eddie Chapple in action." Georgie and Eddie are the two best players on the sixth-grade team. They are also two of the three co-presidents of our class. Diana Mooney is the other. (How we ended up with three presidents is also in my last book.)

The ten of us on the sixth-grade boys' cross-country team have become friends even though we came from three different elementary schools. There are four guys from Goose Cove and four from Bass Rock. Glenn and I are the only ones who went to Rocky Neck.

For practice we usually run about four miles. It's an up-and-down, curvy-swervy path that goes:

1. through the Dogtown woods (there were houses there hundreds of years ago . . . you can see the ruins),

2. around a not-so-small pond (very cool salamanders and frogs . . . I have caught both),

3. out to an abandoned lighthouse (someday I want to climb to the top and look out),

4. back alongside the railroad tracks (Granpa says there used to be lots more trains than now), and finally,

5. between two Little League fields, and then to our school.

Because of the huge rain, this particular practice was miserably fun. It was such a sloppy-gloppy pack of puddles, we were way slower than usual.

I was splooshing along in the middle of the pack, just behind Glenn. Josh Lunares was out in front. His mother is my Spanish teacher.

For the last two weeks, we've been blocked off from finishing our practice runs the usual way. We've had to make a long detour around the field next to the school because big yellow earth-moving machines have been excavating. (Great word! The prefix *ex* means "out" and *cav* comes from the same root as "cave" . . . so it means digging holes.) We're going to get a new middle-school auditorium/media center/bowling alley.

(I'm totally lying about the bowling alley. But wouldn't that be so cool?)

Today there were no workers. The splash-and-bang thunderstorm had canceled everything. Nothing was moving. I didn't know it yet, but this unmanned construction site would turn out to be where my adventure would begin.

I looked at my runner's watch. "We're going to miss the start of the basketball game!" I yelled. "Let's cut across."

"Yeah!" Josh shouted. "Follow me!"

He zigged around a bulldozer and zagged behind a backhoe. We were right behind him. The ground had been all torn up, so everything was puddles or mud or both. It was like running a super-slippery obstacle course. We hurdled over twine strung between stakes in the ground, leaped over two-foot-wide, four-foot-deep trenches, and slogged up and down huge mounds of dirt.

Halfway up the second dirt pile, just a step behind Josh, Glenn slipped and slammed into him, and they both fell forward onto their knees. I tried to scoot around, but I tripped over somebody's legs and toppled chest-first into the mud.

But this was not your usual, everyday mud. Nope.

What if you mixed Super Glue with dirt and water?

Yep. That's what this gunk was. It stuck to everything!

We struggled and slip-slopped back up to our feet, laughing about how muddy we were. Then Josh charged to the top of the mound and yelled, "I'm king of the hill!"

King of the Hill is a game with really simple rules. Whoever stands on top is the king, and everyone else tries to knock him off and take over the throne. Glenn was first to try, but the footing was way too slippery. Josh shoved him when he got close, and Glenn gloop-glooped down the hill on his butt.

"Get Josh!" I shouted, waving an arm to encourage the others to join me as I powered up the mound.

That's when the Mud War began.

Okay, maybe I started it with a perfectly thrown mudball that pegged Josh in the chest, but when he yelled, "Get Cheesie!" Glenn and two other guys totally creamed me. Then the rest of the guys joined in, and the Mud War escalated (Granpa told me that's military talk for "got more violent") into Total Mud War. It became an everybody-throw-at-anybody melee. (An excellent word! It's pronounced MAY-lay. It means a giant, crazy fight going in all directions.)

Mud was flying everywhere! But I made it to the top and was doing okay as King of the Hill, dodging most of the incoming missiles, until Glenn and Josh charged up behind me and smooshed handfuls of mud into my hair.

"Okay! Okay! I give up!" I yelled.

The mud flinging stopped. The Total Mud War was over. I looked around. Every runner on the cross-country team was mudiciously mudified and mudulated.

We were coated!

I don't mean we were just a little bit dirty. Nope.

We were disgustingly dirty. Majorly muddy. Monstrously messy.

And then suddenly I remembered. I yelled, "We're going to be late for the game!"

I ran, and everyone followed me. We jumped over and scooted around the last barriers the construction guys had set up to keep trespassers like us out. Then we were back in the regular, kid-friendly school yard, heading for the boys' locker room to wash up and change clothes. As we neared the gym, we could hear kids cheering from inside.

"It's already started!" Josh yelled.

"Dang!" Glenn wailed.

I didn't want to miss any more of the game against our archrival, Cape Ann Middle School, so I abruptly changed direction.

"Forget the showers!" I shouted. "C'mon!"

Most of the guys kept going, but Josh, Glenn, and I—mud-splattered from our shoes to our scalps—charged through the gym doors, slid past the RLS sixth-grade cheerleaders, and scooted into the first row of the bleachers, where Diana Mooney, Oddny

Thorsdottir, and Lana Shen had been saving seats for us.

In case you haven't read any of my previous books, here's what you need to know about these three girls.

Diana is:

1. very popular,
2. very motivated, and
3. very good at just about anything that needs energy and enthusiasm.

Oddny (who just transferred to RLS from Iceland) is:

1. very tall,
2. very smart, and
3. very much liking Georgie!

Lana is:

1. very speedy (fastest on the girls' cross-country team),
2. very terrific in school (she never tells her grades, but I peeked at her report card . . . straight A's!),
3. very quiet in class (but chatty around her friends and me),

4. sort of almost my friend (she has been in all my previous adventures), but

5. also a little bit bothersome (she wants to know everything I'm doing all the time).

When Lana saw how filthy I was, she squeaked, "Oh my gosh!" and slid closer to Diana and Oddny.

"You guys are disgusting!" Oddny said loudly. (Her father is a fish scientist, an ichthyologist. This fact has nothing to do with my adventure. I just like how it's pronounced: ick-thee-AH-loh-jist.)

I grinned at the girls, which made the drying mud on my cheek crack. It was a weird feeling. I looked up at the scoreboard: Home 6, Visitors 8.

Eddie Chapple had the ball. He totally faked out one of the Cape Ann guards and drained a jump shot from the free throw line to tie the score. I cheered! I bounced up and down. Flecks of mud flew everywhere.

Georgie must have heard me. Sitting on the bench, he turned around, grinned, and waved the hand with the blue forefinger splint.

I waved back. "Go, Georgie!"

Coach Tunavelov (everyone calls him Coach T) sees everything. Even though he was intently watching the action on the court, somehow he just knew Georgie wasn't paying attention. Zingo! One word from Coach T made Georgie spin around, once again totally focused on the game.

We've got a great team, but Cape Ann was just as good. The game was close all the way. We were never ahead, but also never behind by more than five points. With just over one minute left, the score was 28–24. Georgie hadn't played at all. Coach T called a time-out.

Our cheerleaders started a yell, and all of us RLS rooters screamed for our team.

Granpa once told me his favorite high school cheer was:

Hit hat hee,
Kick 'em in the knee!
Hit hat hut,
Kick 'em in the other knee!

I think it's hilarious, but when I suggested it to

Ms. Hammerbord, who's in charge of the cheerlead-ers, she nixed it. (If you don't get it, I explain why it's funny on my website. And you can tell me your favorite cheers.)

Coach T gathered the players around him in a hud-dle. Georgie, who is way taller than anyone else on the team, was talking. I tried to listen—and I was really close—but the cheering was so loud I couldn't hear anything. Coach T said something, and Geor-gie nodded several times. Then the warning buzzer sounded, the team broke out of the huddle, and Geor-gie went over to the scorer's table.

That's strange, I thought as the cheerleaders sat down. I turned to Glenn, who was sitting right next to me. "He's not supposed to play," I said. This was going to be interesting. Georgie's dad had warned him not to reinjure his broken finger.

Glenn nodded. "Perhaps he's going to use only his left hand."

Georgie is right-handed.

"Go for it, Georgie!" a woman shouted.

Georgie smiled and waved at someone behind me.

I turned around. It was Ms. Dinnington, our school nurse. Everyone calls her Ms. D. She and Georgie's father were getting married in a week. Georgie's mother died when he was two. He is really excited about having a stepmother.

The ref blew his whistle again, so Georgie trotted toward our basket, waiting for the action to resume. His position is center, which is almost always the tallest guy on the team. One of our guys threw the ball in to Eddie, who dribbled to the top of the key (he's an excellent ball handler). Georgie moved back and forth under the basket, his left arm up, motioning for the ball. Eddie faked a pass to the side, then zipped the ball really high toward Georgie. The Cape Ann sixth grader guarding him jumped, but Georgie jumped higher. He caught the ball *with just his left hand*, spun around, and laid it into the basket.

28–26.

"Georgie! Georgie! Georgie!" I yelled, and while the Cape Ann team brought the ball up court, everyone near me picked up the chant.

The Cape Ann coach called time-out.

"They're going to have to figure out a way to defend against Georgie!" The cheering was so loud, I had to scream even though Glenn was standing right next to me.

When the game started again, Cape Ann players tossed the ball back and forth, delaying as long as they could.

"Excellent strategy!" Glenn shouted to me. "Using up the time."

I looked at the clock. Only twenty-seven seconds until the game was over! Then good ol' Eddie snagged a bad Cape Ann pass. The RLS fans screamed. This was our chance to tie the score. I looked up at the clock. Just nineteen seconds left. You might think this would be when Eddie would move at super speed.

Nope.

He dribbled carefully up the court toward our basket, setting up the play. He waited patiently until all our guys were in position. He looked left. He looked right. He faked a shot, then zipped that high pass—exactly the same as before—toward Georgie under the basket.

But this time Eddie's throw was a little off. Georgie had to jump to the side and catch the ball with both hands. He dribbled once with his left hand, spun on one foot, and took a shot. But the Cape Ann guy guarding him was ready. He leaped as high as he could, karate-chopping at the ball just as it left Georgie's grasp. But he missed the ball and hit Georgie's hand . . . the one with the broken finger.

What happened next seemed to move in slow motion.

The ball went up.

The referee blew his whistle and threw an arm up into the air. Foul!

The ball hit the backboard

. . . bounced against the rim

. . . rolled all the way around

. . . rolled all the way around again

and fell through.

28–28!

All of us on the RLS side of the gym went cuckoo-bonkers! Diana was so excited, she shoved me. Lana forgot that I was Mr. Mud-Man and grabbed my arm. Oddny kept screaming, "Georgie! Georgie!"

Our fans finally quieted down when they realized Coach T had come out onto the court because a referee had signaled for an official's time-out. I looked up at the clock. 0:03.

"Excuse me, Cheesie," Ms. D said as she came down out of the stands past me and hurried over to the bench.

Coach T was talking to Georgie, who was shaking his head from side to side and holding the hand with the splint. He had a strange look on his face.

"Uh-oh," I said to Glenn. "I think Georgie's injured."

Chapter 2

One Last Shot

Out on the basketball court, all action had stopped. Georgie, Coach T, and Ms. D huddled near the RLS bench, having a conference. Both referees stood nearby, waiting . . . one of them holding the basketball and whistling a tune I couldn't hear.

There weren't a lot of Cape Ann rooters in our gym, but because their team had been leading the whole game up till now, they'd been pretty loud. Now, however, the fans on both sides were quiet.

At first I thought it was babyish and embarrassing for Georgie to have his almost-stepmother holding his hand—because that's what she was doing—but then I realized she wasn't acting like a parent. She was out there because she was our school nurse, checking to see how badly Georgie was hurt.

"What's going on?" Oddny asked me.

I'm not particularly talented at basketball because I'm short, but I know all the rules. "Georgie was fouled," I replied, "so he gets one free throw. If he makes it, we win."

Lana leaned close to listen.

"But if Georgie's hurt," I continued, "Coach T is allowed to take him out of the game and have someone else shoot for him."

"Eddie has the team's best free throw percentage by far," Glenn offered.

"It'll be Eddie for sure," Diana agreed.

I couldn't hear what was going on in the huddle, but of course Georgie could . . . and he's standing right behind me in my bedroom as I'm writing this sentence, so I am going to stop right now and let Georgie tell you.

* * *

Hi! I am Georgie Sinkoff writing this. You can be 100 percent positive I am not as good of a writer as

Cheesie is, so don't go all weird on me when you read what I write. Okay?

First, I'm gonna

(Cheesie is leaning over me, jabbering that *gonna* is not a real word, but too bad. I'm gonna use it anyway!)

Starting over.

First I'm gonna explain that my dad did NOT say I couldn't play. He said just be careful. So I sat on the bench. For almost the whole game. You can't get more careful than that!

I really wanted to play. If you're on a team, who wouldn't? But I didn't complain or whine or anything. Coach T gets majorly annoyed if you beg.

Like Cheesie wrote, it was a really close game. When there was only about a minute to play, Coach T called a time-out. We all huddled up.

"Can you shoot left-handed?" Coach T asked me.

I was kind of surprised by the question. "Not as good as rightie," I said. "But yeah, sort of good."

Coach T stared at me. Probably he was trying to figure out if I was exaggerating or something. "Okay.

You're going in. I want you directly under the basket."

Then he said to Eddie, "Throw him a pass so high, only he can reach it."

So that's what happened, and like Cheesie said, my basket cut the lead to two points. And then we did it again, and I tied the score, but I got fouled.

Cheesie wrote it was like a karate chop. And he was right. Everyone thought that guy had hit my broken finger. But he hadn't. He'd hit me on the wrist. It hurt, but I wasn't hurt. You know what I mean.

Right away Coach T came out onto the court and started talking to the referee about the rules. I heard the ref say "substitution," but that's all I heard because Eddie was whispering smack in my ear, "Tell 'em you're hurt. If you're hurt, Coach T'll get me to shoot the free throw. And I'll definitely sink it. Tell 'em you're hurt."

Eddie is a better free throw shooter than I am. And with a splint on my finger, probably WAY better!

"Do it! Tell Coach T!" Eddie was still whispering. But it seemed really loud. "If you miss, we go into overtime. You want to win, don't you?"

He was right in my face, but he shut up fast when Coach T came back to our huddle. That's when Ms. D came down from the stands and looked at my finger.

Her name is actually Louise Dinnington. I call her Ms. D just like everyone else when she's at RLS being our school nurse. But she's going to be my stepmom in a few days, so when she's at my house I call her Lulu like my dad does. I'm not used to calling her Mom or anything else yet.

They both asked me sort of the same thing at the same time. Coach T: "Can you shoot that free throw?" Lulu: "Are you hurt?" This story is sort of fun to tell, but I'm tired of typing, so I'm gonna (HA!) turn this computer back to Cheesie and he's gonna (DOUBLE HA!) finish. But first I want to say hi to my three older brothers. (And Cheesie, you better not take this out, because you know they're going to be in this book later in the story!)

Hi, Jokie. (His real name is Joseph Keith.)

Hi, Fed. (His real name is Fred, but I couldn't say it right when I was a kittle lid. HA!)

Hi, Marlon. (His real name is Marlon. DOUBLE HA!)

And there's one more thing all of you guys reading this should know. Cheesie definitely likes Lana. Don't deny it, Cheesie! You know it's true. So if you delete this, I will grab you when you're for sure not watching and stick your head in the nearest toilet!

Okay. I'm done. Now back to your regularly scheduled Cheesie.

* * *

(I won't delete it, but it's totally not true. And that's all I'm going to write about it.)

* * *

The score was 28–28 with only three seconds left in the game.

Georgie knew Eddie was sort of, kind of, maybe

right about how to win. Georgie wasn't actually injured, but if he *lied* and told Coach T he was hurt, Eddie would sub for him and shoot his free throw. Eddie is really good. He'd probably make it, and then we'd win. And if Eddie missed, no one would ever blame Georgie.

But if Georgie told the *truth* . . .

Everything would depend on him.

I knew what Georgie would do . . . and I was right.

I saw Georgie shake his head, then sort of shoulder Eddie aside as he turned to face Coach T. I saw Georgie's face for only a second, but that was all I needed. When Georgie gets nervous, his eyebrows waggle up and down. This time?

Nope.

No waggle.

He looked right at me and Lana and Oddny and gave a big thumbs-up with his splinted hand. The ref blew his whistle. And both teams trotted back onto the court.

Huge cheers went up from both sides. Georgie took

the ball from one of the refs and stood with his toes right up to the free throw line. He was facing away from me, so I couldn't see his face. I stared at the 11 on his back. Georgie had chosen that number when Coach T handed out uniforms.

"Some people think eleven's a lucky number," I'd told him when he showed me his new uniform.

"One of those people is me," he'd replied with a grin.

Georgie bounced the ball a couple of times, lined up the shot, then lofted the ball toward the basket.

His free throw was short. Way short.

A sound kind of like a loud moan came out of the RLS fans.

Georgie's shot hit the front of the rim and bounced straight up and straight back. Georgie charged forward. He jumped higher than anyone, controlled the rebound with his left hand, and tipped the ball up.

It swished through just as the buzzer sounded.

We won 30–28!

Operation Three

Teetering on the Edge

Everyone called him Big Eleven.

His real name was something else, "but eleven is my lucky number, and that's what I'm gonna be called." He was a big man . . . the biggest soldier in our regiment. Solid. Tough. If I had to pick one totally dependable guy who could pull us out of whatever predicament we were in, I'd always go with Big Eleven.

We'd been on a mission in unfriendly territory. Had a couple of close calls. Traded a few shots with the Kaypan forces. But neither side had achieved any significant victories. If someone had asked me, I'd have said the good guys and the bad guys were tied.

All we had to do was cross over the mountain the local people called Kin Guf Daheel and then we'd be back at base camp. But the weather had been miserably wet, and the dirt road was treacherous. Sloppy. Narrow. Winding. Steep.

Big Eleven had been hurt in a previous battle, but it wasn't real bad. He didn't complain or ask for any special treatment, so Captain Tuna put him in the lead vehicle. I was right behind.

We headed up the mountain. It was quiet.

Too quiet, I thought.

Just as we reached the narrowest section of the climb, the road in front of me collapsed into a huge, thundering mud slide. My front wheels dropped into the emptiness that used to be a road, and my truck tipped onto its side.

My windows were covered with mud, but I could tell I was in big trouble. My vehicle was half over the edge. I struggled to get out, but the weight of the avalanche on the door was too much. I started to climb through a smashed window, but my shifting weight caused the truck to teeter. I stopped moving . . . and so did the truck.

I looked down. Below me was a sheer drop into a rocky, kiss-it-all-goodbye canyon.

But on the other side of the now-broken road stood Big Eleven. He gave me a thumbs-up with his bad hand, then pulled his arm back to throw me a rope.

* * *

My dad and I like watching war movies. Granpa doesn't. He says they bring back too many bad memories. My mom thinks they're too violent. She wouldn't let me watch any until I was ten.

While I was writing about the end of our basketball game, I started thinking how sports contests are like battles. So I decided to see if I could turn the Cape Ann—RLS game into a war story.

You probably guessed Kaypan was Cape Ann, Captain Tuna was Coach T, and the karate chop to Georgie's hand turned into the mud slide. And I shouldn't have to tell you what Kin Guf Daheel was. (Just sound it out.) Mrs. Wikowitz, my English teacher, helped me come up with the idea of symbolizing the tie game with the truck hanging over the edge.

It was hard to write a war story, because I don't know very much about war. My dad helped me. He was in the Navy. He advised me to call this Operation Three instead of chapter 3 because it sounds more military.

I read Operation Three to a bunch of my classmates at lunch. If you can picture a string of Christmas tree lights with one bulb that doesn't light up . . . that bulb is Alex Welch. He was the only guy who didn't know who Big Eleven was.

I bet you did.

Chapter 4

My Adventure Begins

By the time I showered all the mud off me and got into my street clothes, everyone except Georgie and Coach T had left the boys' locker room.

"Great game, Georgie," Coach T said as we waved goodbye. "Starting tomorrow, we're going to practice that left-hand shooting. You're going to be a double threat."

Usually we bike to and from school, but because of the morning thunderstorm . . . you remember . . . Georgie and I had to walk home.

"That's where we played King of the Hill." I pointed at a large mound.

Georgie took a quick glance around the deserted

construction site, then hopped over the low tape barrier.

"What're you doing?" I called after him.

"I've always wanted to sit in one of these," Georgie said as he climbed onto a huge yellow Caterpillar excavator.

(When I was little, I had a whole set of toy Caterpillar earth-moving machines. They're called Cats, and I learned the names and functions of every one of them. If you want to see some, I put photos on my website.)

"I don't think you ought to do that," I warned, following him into the construction site.

"I'm not going to turn it on or anything," Georgie countered, climbing into the cab and plunking down in the driver's seat. He grabbed the control levers and began making growling engine noises. "It would be so cool to actually operate one of these," he said, pausing his motor sounds to speak to me. "You know, dig holes and pile dirt into gigantic dump trucks."

That got my imagination going, and I stood next to the big machine, listening to Georgie's noises and picturing the two of us in hard hats. If he was going to pretend to operate the excavator, I'd be the foreman in charge of the job.

"Come on, Sinkoff! Pick up the pace!" I yelled. "You've got a line of empty trucks backed up all the way around the block." I waved my arms like I was angry. "If you can't get that Cat movin' dirt any

faster, I'll get a pro in here who can."

Georgie and I have been playing these kind of pretend games forever. He knew instantly what I was doing.

"No problem, boss," he replied. "I had a breakdown with my hopper gripper dingle-dangle. But I got everything working now."

(There's no such thing as a hopper gripper dingle-dangle. Georgie was just making stuff up.)

The excavator noises coming out of Georgie's mouth got louder. He moved his hands back and forth across the controls. I looked up at the bucket at the end of the giant digging arm, then down into the nearby trench, imagining it scooping up great mouthfuls of dirt.

And that's when I saw something sort of shiny sticking out of the mud about two feet down the side of the trench wall.

It wasn't like I got instantly excited. I didn't shout "Eureka!" or "Leaping Kooga-Mooga!" or anything.

Nope.

I didn't know what it was yet. I just walked to the edge of the trench, leaned over, and stared.

Chapter 5

The Thingie

"What're you looking at?" Georgie shouted from his seat up in the excavator.

"There's some kind of thingie down there," I replied.

"What kind of thingie?"

I didn't answer. I was thinking, *Okay, here goes. I guess I'm going to get all muddy again.* I didn't care. I jumped into the trench.

Bad idea.

I landed with a huge *SQUISH!* The bottom was like quicksand. I immediately sank halfway up to my knees. I tried to lift one foot.

Nope. I couldn't move.

(Hey! You know what? I hadn't thought of it until now, but I bet I was unconsciously thinking of this two chapters ago when I wrote about my soldier truck getting mud-slided during Operation Three. It's weird how my mind works.)

The trench was over four feet deep. I am not much taller. And since I had sunk in about ten inches, my eyes were below the top of the trench.

"Georgie! Help! I'm stuck."

I couldn't see him get down from the excavator, but pretty soon he appeared next to the trench. He gave a long look down at me, then smiled in a devilish way.

"I gotta get home," he said. "Goo luck!"

Then he disappeared.

"Georgieeee!" I yelled.

A few seconds later he reappeared, laughing like crazy. "Goo luck. Get it?"

"Very funny," I replied. "C'mon, pull me out." I lifted my arms.

Georgie grabbed me around my wrists, and I grabbed his. Just as he started to pull, I yelled, "Wait!"

I had forgotten the whole reason I had jumped into the trench. The thingie I was curious about was still there, sticking out of the dirt, right in front of me . . . just about even with my belly button. I dug it out of the sidewall of the trench, knocked most of the dirt off it, and held it up for Georgie to see.

"What is it?" Georgie asked.

"Dunno," I replied. It was a flat, mostly tarnished, brass-colored metal ring with a bunch of strange markings around the edge. It was about the size of my cell phone. I stuck the thingie into my jacket pocket and grabbed Georgie's wrists. He gave a huge pull, but my shoes were so deep into the mud he couldn't budge me.

"Try again," I said. "But pull me to the side, and I'll try to lift just my right foot."

I leaned. He pulled. It worked.

Sort of.

My foot popped out . . . but without my shoe! I

stood on one leg. I bet I looked like a really awkward flamingo.

Georgie looked at me flapping my foot-in-a-sock all around and laughed, but then he said, "Hold it. I'll find you something to stand on."

He disappeared from view. I balanced on one leg, reached down with my hand, and dug around for my shoe. I could feel it, but no way could I pull it out.

Georgie reappeared holding his backpack and three short wooden stakes with a bunch of twine tied to them. He pulled his stinky gym clothes out of his backpack.

"What're you doing?" I asked.

"I have to wash these anyway," he said. He pulled the twine off the stakes, then stuffed the stakes and all his other gym clothes inside his RLS T-shirt and tied it all up.

The leg I was standing on was getting wiggly-wobbly tired.

"Hurry up," I said.

He held on to one end of the twine and handed me the bundle.

"The wood junk will make this kind of solid," Georgie said, "and the string is so I can pull my stuff back up after I get you out."

"Good thinking," I said, lowering the shirt bundle to the bottom of the trench. I carefully placed my foot on it and slowly transferred my weight onto it. It squished into the mud, but not very deep.

"I'm ready," I said.

Georgie dug his feet in, bent over, and stuck his arms down to me. I grabbed his wrists again.

He rocked back and forth as he said, "One . . . two . . . ," and when he said, "THREE!" he yanked.

Georgie is really strong. He pulled so hard that:

1. I flew up over the edge, sliding on my chest in the dirt, ending up halfway out of the trench.

2. He flew backward, sliding on his butt, ending up halfway to the King of the Hill dirt pile!

3. I lost my other shoe.

That's when I smelled cigarette smoke. (Nobody in my house smokes. I think it is a disgusting habit.)

I crawled forward and peeked around the dirt pile. Two men were on the other side of the construction site, standing near a car that hadn't been there when we arrived. One was a big guy with red hair and a huge belly. He was smoking a cigarette and holding a clipboard. The other man was facing away and pointing at our school. He said something about the trench and pipes, then started to turn toward us, so I ducked back down.

"I bet we're not supposed to be here," I whispered.

"Duh," Georgie replied softly, tugging his muddy bundle of stinky gym clothes out of the trench.

"Let's go," I said.

"What about your shoes?"

"Forget 'em. My mom said they were getting too small for me. She's buying me new ones anyway."

Hunched over in a low crouch, the two of us snooked (*sneaked* and *looked* at the same time) out the far side of the construction site without being seen. But to get home, we had to walk on the sidewalk right next to the two men, and the redheaded guy must have noticed how muddy we both were, and I know he looked at my shoeless feet suspiciously, but we weren't doing anything wrong (right then), so I smiled and waved.

It took a while to walk home, but when we got . . .

> *to where my street*
> *and Georgie's meet,*
> *I was really beat*
> *and my poor feet*
> *felt cold as sleet.*
> *I needed heat,*
> *and I wanted to eat.*
> *I think it's neat for "eet" to repeat.*

(Don't worry. That will be the only terrible poem in this whole book. I promise.)

When we got to the corner where our streets diverge (cool word . . . it means split apart in separate directions), we headed toward my house. Georgie almost always hung with me after school waiting for his dad to get home from work, but recently, because Ms. D and his father were getting married, sometimes she came to his house after school. We hadn't taken two steps when her car pulled up near us.

"Cheesie, where are your shoes? Omigosh! You two are filthy. Come with me."

In less than six minutes (I am not exaggerating!), Ms. D had:

1. called Granpa and told him where we were,

2. shoved us into Georgie's bathroom and told us to strip down and shower up,

3. thrown our muddy clothes into the washer,

4. ordered sushi for dinner,

5. chased a pair of raccoons out of the kitchen, and

6. put a tray of chocolate chip cookies into the oven, which by the time we got out of the shower were smelling up the house something terrific!

(I lied about the raccoons . . . but I did not lie about the cookies!)

Since my clothes were in the dryer, when I got out of the shower I had to wear Georgie's slippers and a pair of his much-too-big pajamas.

Ms. D is so funny. When she saw me holding up the pants to keep them from falling, she grabbed a roll of packing tape and zipped it around my waist like a belt. Then she rolled up my sleeves and pant legs and taped those, too. I made crinkly sounds when I moved, but it worked!

A few minutes later, Georgie's father walked in with the sushi, gave Ms. D a big hug and a kiss, then grabbed both me and Georgie up out of our chairs and swung us around. Normally he is a not-so-excitable guy. But I guess because he was getting married in less than a week, he was super happy or something.

The conversation at dinner was completely boring. The adults talked about wedding this and wedding that. Georgie and I concentrated on chewing. (Lots of kids think raw fish is too weird to eat. I am doing a survey. Please go to my website and tell me if you like sushi.) We had just begun seriously working on the cookies when the front door opened.

Everyone jumped up from the table, and there was nothing but noise and chatter and chaos for the next fifteen minutes.

It was Georgie's three brothers: Joe, Fred, and Marlon. Each was accompanied by a female:

1. Joseph Keith (Jokie), who is twenty-seven, came with his wife, Charlotte.

2. Fred (Fed), twenty-four, came with his girlfriend, Ava.

3. Marlon (Marlon), twenty-two, brought his cat, Squirrel . . . named that because she likes to climb trees. But not right then because she was hugely pregnant.

I wish I had a brother. All I have is June, my very treacherous, devious, unpleasant older sister, whom, as you probably know, I call Goon.

After Georgie got a huge number of hugs and noogie airlifts (knuckle-clunks on the head), his brothers asked him a trillion questions about school and sports and girlfriends (I couldn't believe it . . . he actually mentioned Oddny's name!). I was a little embarrassed to be wearing guy-jantic, taped-up paja- mas, so I mostly just hid out and petted Squirrel.

"She's going to have her puppies any day now," Marlon told me.

I gave him a squinty-evil-eye. He grinned and gently pulled Squirrel's tail. She looked at him and purred. Most cats hate to have their tails pulled. I guess he trained her to like it. Or maybe she's weird.

I could tell Georgie wanted to hang out with his brothers, but after a while everyone sort of ignored him, once again talking about only wedding glurg. (This is another word I made up. I use it to mean anything that clogs things up.)

"Boring," Georgie muttered to me. He gently pulled Squirrel's tail. "You are a very fat kitty," he told her. She didn't seem to mind.

Then his brothers lugged tons of luggage in from the car, and Mr. Sinkoff told Georgie, "If you have any homework or stuff you need for school, get it now. You'll be sleeping at Cheesie's for the next few days."

Georgie trotted upstairs to get what he needed. Ms. D took my clothes out of the dryer, folded them, and handed them to me in a plastic bag.

"I found this in the pocket of your jacket," she said to me, holding out the thingie. "What is it?"

I had completely forgotten about it! "I don't exactly know," I said. "Georgie and I found it."

"It looks very interesting," she said as Georgie

came downstairs. "Let me know when you figure it out."

Then she gave Georgie a hug.

"You really like her, don't you?" I asked as we hopped over the creek and went through the won't-close gate into my backyard.

Georgie nodded.

I put my arm around his shoulder. "You're lucky," I said. "She's going to be a very cool stepmother."

Chapter 6

The Mack Supreme Court

The first person to see me when I walked in my back door was Goon. She took one look at me in Georgie's taped-up pajamas and floppy slippers and began laughing hysterically.

"What a jerk! You look stupider than stupid. What are you? A package the mailman rejected? A Christmas present nobody wanted? You look like something a homeless hobo would throw up on. Omigosh, I am so glad my friend Donna already left. It's bad enough that you go to the same school as I do. Omigosh, if she'd seen you dressed like that, I'd be too embarrassed to be seen in public."

"Are you finished?" I said when she finally took

a breath. "What you don't know is, the reason I'm dressed like I am is because I got all muddy when I found this." I shoved the thingie in her face and then pulled it away.

She was instantly curious. "What is that? Where'd you find it?"

"Wouldn't you like to know," I said just loud enough for her to hear . . . and then Georgie and I dashed out. We sped past Granpa, who was watching the baseball playoffs on television, and zipped up the stairs and into my room. I shut my door.

"So yeah . . . your sister's right. What is it? I mean really," Georgie asked.

"I don't know," I replied. "But I think it's really old and maybe valuable."

I held it up for both of us to examine.

"I think it's brass," I said. "You know, like they make keys out of."

"Could be part of some kind of award or medal," Georgie suggested. "Like a general would wear and there used to be a star or a ruby or something that hung in the middle?"

I counted the triangular markings around the edge. Thirty-two. Every fourth one had some scratchings next to it.

"Do you think this is writing?" I wondered aloud, my finger pointing to one of the scratchings.

"Could be an *E*," Georgie replied.

Just then Goon knocked on my open door and asked, "May I come in?"

One of the rules in our house that neither of us breaks (well, almost never) is we can't go in the other kid's bedroom without permission.

"No way," I said.

"I'd like to see what you have," she continued, acting all polite and nice.

I was not fooled. "Get lost," I said.

I heard her stomp off to her room and slam the door.

"Let's go ask my dad about this thingie," I said.

"Okay," Georgie said, "but you can't tell him where we found it."

I must have had *Why not?* all over my face, because Georgie continued, "I am totally sure my dad will kill me if he finds out I was fooling around on a backhoe."

"It was an excavator," I said.

"Whatever," Georgie muttered. Then he brightened and said, "Your father might actually know about this. He reads a lot about history, doesn't he?"

Actually that's exactly what my father was doing at that exact moment. He was lying on his bed reading a book about the Civil War.

"I prefer reading in a supine position because then I can remove my foot," he once told me.

There are two things in that last sentence that might confuse you:

1. *Supine* (soo-PINE) means lying flat on your back. If you're flat on your stomach, that's lying prone. (Those are two excellent words to use in school reports. Your teacher will love them . . . I promise.)

2. My father had to have his right foot amputated when he was twenty. He was in the U.S. Navy on an aircraft carrier, and somebody goofed and dropped a huge bomb when they were loading it onto a jet. It didn't explode, but it squashed his foot. Can you imagine how much that must have hurt? He doesn't get the least bit upset when he talks about it now, but he says when it happened, he passed out. Now he wears a prosthetic (artificial) foot, and he likes to take it off whenever he can.

"Hey, Pop," I said from the doorway. "Can I bother you with a question?"

"Sure."

"Actually," I continued, "it's more like advice than a question."

"Okay." He plopped his book facedown and sat up. "Shoot."

"So . . . Georgie and I found something." I was holding it behind my back. "We don't know what it is, but it looks like it might be really old and probably important or valuable or something."

"Sounds interesting," he said.

"Yeah, kinda. But there's a problem." I glanced at Georgie. He was nodding. "I need to make a deal with you," I continued. "I'll show you the thingie we found, and you can give us whatever advice you have, but we can only tell you *most* of how and where we found it."

"Sounding even more interesting now," Dad said, sitting up straighter. "I'll accept your deal on one condition. Those parts of the story you decide to leave out cannot involve . . . one, actual or potential bodily harm . . . two, law-breaking activities . . . or three, meanness or disrespect to others."

(You can probably tell where I get my ability to make lists.)

"One moment," I said holding up a finger. I turned around and shoved Georgie into the hallway.

"What do you think?" I asked him.

"Nothing we did was mean or disrespectful," Georgie said soft enough so Dad wouldn't hear. "And no way I'd hurt myself climbing on that backhoe."

"Excavator," I said.

"Whatev—" Georgie said.

I cut him off. "It's what he said about law-breaking activities that's the problem."

Just then Goon came out of her bedroom, gave us a hard stare, and went into the bathroom.

"I don't think we actually broke any laws," Georgie whispered.

"How about trespassing?" I countered.

"I didn't see any Keep Out signs."

"Yeah, maybe," I sort of agreed. "But everybody knows that place was off-limits or private property or something."

"It's school property," Georgie said with a bit of

a smile. "And we're middle school students. That's gotta be good for something."

I stood there thinking. Georgie just stared at me. Goon came out of the bathroom holding a hairbrush. She stopped for a moment, stuck out her tongue, and then went into her bedroom. Sometimes it's hard to believe she's a teenager.

"Okay," I said. "Maybe you're sort of right. We weren't supposed to be in the construction site, but maybe there's no actual law against it. It's not like we were sneaking into a bank vault or blowing up a secret laboratory."

"Right!" Georgie said a bit too loudly. Then, softly, "It's like the difference between a little fib . . . which is maybe what we did . . . and a big huge lie."

I wrinkled my forehead and gave a half nod. I wasn't completely sure our analysis was correct. But we needed advice, so we went back into my dad's bedroom and showed him the thingie.

"I found it in some kind of a trench that was being dug somewhere," I told him as he examined it.

"Where?" he asked.

"That's the part I can't tell you," I replied. My stomach felt kind of gurgly. I think I was getting a little bit nervous.

"You boys are sort of like prospectors who found a large gold nugget that might lead to a very big bonanza . . . and you don't want to give away the location, huh?"

Georgie and I were nodding when Mom asked, "What's this about a bonanza? What location?" She had been in her bathroom and had obviously over-heard the end of our conversation.

"Look at this, Edie." Dad handed Mom the thingie. "What do you think this doohickey is?"

"It's definitely not a doohickey," I said, trying to control the conversation. I know my mother. I absolutely knew what was coming next.

"Where'd you find it?" she asked.

Yep. I knew it. I turned to Dad with a please-help-me look on my face.

He gave Mom a smiley look. "The boys and I made a deal. Kind of an ask-me-no-questions—"

"Nope," Mom said sternly.

"—and I'll-tell-you-no-lies kind of a deal," Dad continued.

"I did not agree to any such thing," Mom said. "Where did you find it?"

"Dad?" I pleaded.

Goon now butted in. How she snuck up behind me, I don't know.

"I saw him come in with whatever that thing-amajig is. I bet he stole it." There was an evil sort of happiness in her voice.

Dad swung his legs over the side of the bed and reached for his fake foot. Clearly this conversation was not over.

"Georgie?" Mom looked straight at him.

Georgie's eyebrows started waggling up and down, which is a sure sign he was getting anxious. "We, um, me and Cheesie, I uh—"

And then, out of nowhere, Granpa was at the door. I guess the baseball game was over or boring or something.

"Sounds to me like the lad is taking the Fifth Amendment," Granpa said.

Georgie looked at Granpa and nodded rapidly. He knew what that meant because we just learned about the Fifth Amendment in Mrs. Wikowitz's class. It is part of the Bill of Rights to the U.S. Constitution, and it says, "No person . . . shall be compelled in any criminal case to be a witness against himself."

"You don't have to answer the question, Georgie," Granpa announced. "And it appears, from what I heard coming up the stairs—and none of you were very quiet—that I need to call the Mack Supreme Court into immediate session."

"Yes!" I almost shouted.

"Okay with me," Mom said. "I'll be the prosecutor." She sat down on the bed next to Dad.

"Good idea, Pop," my father said, strapping on his foot. "I'll be the defense attorney."

Goon shoved her way past me and sat next to Mom on the bed. "I get to be the executioner."

If you read my earlier books, you know we have lots of Mack Family Traditions. The Mack Supreme Court is one of them. (Also our squinty-evil-eye and musical belching. I have a very strange family.)

"Start us off, Cheesie," Granpa told me in a loud whisper.

I stood up straight and announced in a very official voice, "Hear ye! Hear ye! The Mack Supreme Court is now in session. Honorable Chief Justice Melvyn Bud Mack presiding."

Georgie looked confused, which was pretty understandable because he had never been at a Mack Supreme Court before.

"The prosecution may now begin," Granpa said, pointing to Mom.

My mother is really smart. She stood, smiled in a sneaky way, and then said, "Your Honor, instead of the Fifth Amendment, I offer the witnesses a challenge. I will ask four questions which they must answer with lies. If they succeed in lying to every question, I will ask nothing further. If, however, either of them tells the truth even once, they must tell the truth to all my succeeding questions."

From his expression, it was obvious Granpa had no idea what Mom was up to. Neither did I.

"The Mack Supreme Court finds the request interesting," Granpa said, then turned to Dad. "Is that acceptable to your clients?"

Dad gave me a questioning look. I thought for a moment, then pulled Georgie next to me and whispered, "All we have to do is answer every question wrong. It'll be easy. Okay?"

"Okay," Georgie whispered back. He still looked a little confused.

I nodded to Dad.

"My clients agree to lie," he said.

Mom stood, paced around the bedroom as if she were thinking hard, and then spun on one foot and pointed at Georgie so fast he actually jumped.

"Georgie Sinkoff . . . how much is two plus two?"

Georgie's eyes darted from Mom to me. I could tell he thought it was some kind of trick.

"Answer the question," Dad said softly.

"Umm . . ." Georgie hesitated. "Umm . . . five and one-half."

"Very good, Mr. Sinkoff," Mom said.

Georgie looked at me. We grinned at each other.

Mom tapped a finger to her lips, looked out the bedroom window, then turned around slowly and asked me in a very accusative voice, "Ronald Mack, where were you last August sixteenth in the afternoon?"

That was easy. August 16 was my birthday, and it was the last day of summer camp. I looked around the room. Here's what I saw:

1. Granpa had a stone-faced expression, looking exactly like a very stern judge.

2. Mom was pointing a finger at me, looking exactly like a prosecuting attorney quizzing a defendant.

3. Dad was giving me a squinty-evil-eye, looking exactly like my dad when he tries to make me laugh.

4. Georgie was smiling a little bit, but I could tell he was nervous, because his eyebrows were still waggling.

5. Goon was staring straight at me, silently mouthing, *Your birthday . . . your birthday . . . your birthday.*

I stared right back at my sister. She was trying to

hypnotize me into telling the truth, but I saw a way for a Point Battle victory.

"Oh, yes," I said. "August sixteenth. That was when my sister fell off the stage at her ballet recital, landed in the orchestra pit, and got her entire head stuck inside a tuba."

Goon swung a fist at me, but I am much more agile than she is. She missed, clunked her hand against Mom's bedpost, and squealed a whiny "Owww!"

Sort of ducking behind Granpa, I pretended to be

offended. "Jump back, Junie! Where's your sense of humor? It's supposed to be a lie. Are you upset because maybe it's actually true? Did you really stick your head inside a tuba?"

She swung at me again, but Dad grabbed her arm as it flew past him.

"Cool it, kids!" he said sternly.

Goon's face turned red. Four points for me. I increased my lead. 739–694!

Mom, still acting like the prosecutor, had mostly ignored Goon's interruption. She turned to Georgie. "Mr. Sinkoff, what event is taking place this coming weekend?"

Another easy one. Georgie's father and Ms. D were getting married on Sunday, and we were all invited.

Georgie smiled. "At midnight on Saturday night, Cheesie and I will turn into werewolves."

I laughed out loud.

Georgie kept going. He was having fun lying. "And then we'll run through Gloucester howling at the moon and everything."

I howled, "Ow-ooooo!"

Mom nodded, then asked me, "Was that my third question?"

"Yes," I answered.

"Thank you for that surprisingly truthful answer," she said. "You lose. Now tell me where and how you found this so-called thingie."

"Huh?" I asked.

My mother turned to Granpa. "Would Your Honor please instruct the witness he must tell the truth to all further questions?"

Then it hit me. "Mom! You tricked me!"

"I certainly did," she said with a smile.

(I think you can figure out what Mom did, but if you don't know how she tricked me, go to my website. I let Mom put up a page explaining everything.)

Goon began laughing hysterically. It was a totally fake laugh.

"Quit it!" I shouted. (I had lost control, and this was going to hurt me in the Point Battle . . .)

"Loser!" she yelled, jumping up and down and waving a two-finger *L* in my face. (. . . but Goon overdid it.)

"June!" Dad said sternly. "Out!" (So when Dad sent her to her room . . .)

"But—" she said. (. . . and she argued,)

"Now!" Dad insisted. (I decided it was a tie. That meant no points. It was still 739–694.)

Goon stomped away. Moments later I heard her bedroom door almost slam. (Neither of us actually slams doors. In our house there is an instant Mom-enforced penalty for that.)

Then it was quiet.

Until Mom gave me a hard look. "The truth, Ronald. Now."

I had no choice. I confessed. I told her everything Georgie and I did at the construction site.

Mom was upset. "You could've gotten seriously injured playing around all that big equipment."

"But they didn't," Dad said.

"Grounded for a year would be the right punishment!" Goon shouted from her bedroom. (I guess her door wasn't shut all the way.)

"Cool it, June," Dad said loudly and firmly. "Come on, everyone. Let's keep our eyes on the ball here.

I think what Georgie and Cheesie found might be really important."

Granpa slapped his hand down on a dresser and announced loudly, "I have heard enough. The Mack Supreme Court has made its decision. These boys must take this whatever-it-is to the Gloucester Museum. The guy who runs the place is Bob Hernandes, one of my fishing buddies. If he thinks it's important, the crime will be overlooked in the interest of historical discovery. Otherwise, bread and water for a week."

He gave me a squinty-evil-eye.

"Or whatever punishment the prosecutor"—Granpa pointed at Mom—"decides is appropriate."

Mom nodded.

"Okay then," Granpa continued. "Sentence postponed until tomorrow."

Chapter 7

Tragabigzanda

(I know that looks like a totally bogus title for a chapter, but keep reading. . . .)

The next morning, as Georgie and I came downstairs wearing our school backpacks, Granpa had our breakfasts ready, but he wouldn't let us sit and eat. He was standing by the door, holding sandwiches, napkins, a couple of juice boxes, and two apples.

"Big hurry!" he shouted. "Get over here and open up!"

Like baby birds, we opened our mouths, and one second later we were gripping melted cheese sandwiches with our teeth, our hands were full of apples and juice boxes, and he was rushing us out to his car.

(You probably have noticed that if you have
something tasty that's halfway in your mouth, but
you can't bite it or chew it, you will definitely drool.
In fact, by the time we got our seat belts fastened,
and I was finally able to set down my apple and juice
box and grab the sandwich, I was drooling down
my chin.)

We were at the Gloucester Museum in less than three minutes. My sandwich was only half-eaten, and I had just taken my first apple bite.

"Leave it!" Granpa said. "This guy Hernandes is a very busy man."

Granpa was really moving! He charged through the museum's back door with Georgie and me running after him. I straight-armed the door as I sucked the last of my juice box and, still following Granpa, spotted a trash basket and lofted a perfect shot. I watched my empty juice box tumble end over end, heading right for . . .

And I crashed into a woman I hadn't even noticed.

She dropped the notebook she'd been writing in.

"Sorry," I blurted. I quickly retrieved her notebook and handed it back. I actually expected to be yelled at or scolded or something, but the woman smiled.

"No harm done," she said softly.

Now, don't get all weird on me because of what I'm going to write next, but the people who publish my books tell me I need to describe the characters in my stories, so I am just being honest and not mushy or romantic or any of that gunk, but this woman was beautiful. I'm not going to tell you about her hair or eye color or anything else. Just beautiful. That's enough.

"What're those?" I mumbled, pointing at the rock-looking objects she'd been inspecting on a table.

She smiled again. "This is a Wampanoag moose-hide scraper. These are Agawam arrowheads."

I pointed at a little white one. "Pretty small for an arrowhead," I said.

She kept smiling. "It's called a bird point. Used for—"

"Hunting birds!" I said, feeling very smart for a second. (But now that I am writing this, I am thinking, *DUH, Mr. Obvious!*)

"Cheesie!" Georgie shouted from somewhere.

I ran down the hall. Georgie and Granpa were just stepping into an office. At a desk, a big gray beard (with a man behind it) was banging away at a computer.

No lie! That was my first impression.

The beard belonged to Mr. Hernandes (I could tell because of the nameplate on his desk). It was the biggest, widest beard I had ever seen. He gave Granpa a stern look. "You're late, Bud."

"Your clock is wrong, Bob," Granpa said. "And you get uglier every time I see you."

Mr. Hernandes stood up slowly and gave Granpa a really dirty look. "You'd have to come see me fifty more times before I'd be as ugly as you." His beard

was so bushy, you could barely see his lips move when he talked.

They glared at each other like they were total enemies. I was completely confused. I looked at Georgie. His eyes were wide.

Granpa suddenly smiled broadly and stuck out his hand. "Bob, you batty old buzzard! How the heck are you?"

Mr. Hernandes grinned from inside his huge beard and shook Granpa's hand. "I'm as mean and nasty as I ever was. It's good to see you, Bud."

Suddenly I understood. My Granpa is bad-tempered, cantankerous, contrary, crabby, cranky, critical, cross, crotchety, grouchy, grumpy, irritable, ornery, peevish, prickly, quarrelsome, snappish, and vinegary.

And I guess he has some friends who are just like him.

(The words I used to describe Granpa are in alphabetical order because I got them out of a thesaurus, which sounds like it's some kind of dinosaur but is actually a collection of synonyms. It is an excellent online tool when you are writing a report or a story or something.)

Granpa turned to Georgie and me. "Show him what you got."

I pulled the thingie out of my jacket pocket and handed it across the desk. Mr. Hernandes sat back down in his chair and peered at it closely, turning it over and over in his hands. Then he fumbled around in a desk drawer, took out a magnifying glass, and examined it even closer.

"If you want my opinion . . . ," Granpa said, breaking the silence.

"I don't," Mr. Hernandes muttered, his eye peering closely through the magnifying glass. "Elizabeth!" he shouted. "Please come in here!"

The woman I had bumped into appeared in the doorway.

"Take a look," Mr. Hernandes said, holding out our thingie and the magnifying glass to the woman. "What do you make of this?"

She nodded to Granpa and Georgie and smiled at me. "Hello again."

I am not good at guessing women's ages (and my mom told me I should never ask), but I think she was probably in her thirties.

Mr. Hernandes continued, "This is Professor Elizabeth Solescu. She researches American history and archaeology at Harvard. She's my daughter." He looked very proud. Then he told her our names.

Granpa immediately stood up and actually sort of bowed to Professor Solescu. I didn't know what to do, so I just smiled. She smiled back and took the thingie and the magnifying glass from her father. He looked at me and Georgie and tugged his beard. "Where'd you find this, boys?"

I told them everything about the construction site. But I also remember thinking, *If he were fatter and jollier, Mr. Hernandes could be Santa Claus.* He and his daughter listened intently, she inspecting the thingie, he stroking his beard and nodding the whole time.

When I finished explaining, Granpa interjected, "I think it's part of a ship's compass. And a real old one, too."

"You're quite close, Mr. Mack," Professor Solescu said to Granpa. "It's part of a compass, all right, but it's not the kind you'd find on a ship. It's the kind someone would bring ashore when they were mapping or exploring." Then she looked at Georgie and me. "Have you boys ever heard of Pocahontas?"

Of course we had. Who hasn't?

"And John Smith? He was the fellow the chief was going to kill, but Pocahontas put her head next to his so he wouldn't get his brains bashed in. Remember him?"

"Sure," Georgie said. "I saw the movie."

"Me too," I said.

Professor Solescu seemed pleased with our answers. "That was down in what's now Virginia. A few years later, in 1614, after Captain John Smith had been back to England, he came here. Right here where we are today. Most people don't know that."

I certainly didn't . . . and we studied explorers last year, in fifth grade.

Professor Solescu then told us, with lots of detail, what happened here about four hundred years ago.

Her story was really interesting. I looked at the clock on the wall. We were definitely going to be late for Mrs. Wikowitz's homeroom, but this was worth it.

It would take about three chapters to write everything that she said, and I'm guessing you'd rather know how the compass thingie we found made me and Georgie famous. So here comes a much shorter version.

Captain John Smith came to New England looking to trade with the Indians. Except New England was called North Virginia back then. He drew a map of this area. It wasn't all that accurate, but he did name a few places. What we now call Cape Ann (which is where Gloucester is), he named Tragabigzanda.

(I know . . . I know . . . that's a really weird name. That's why I thought it would make a terrific chapter title.)

Captain John Smith chose that name because a few years before Pocahontas saved him from getting his head smashed in in Virginia, he fought in a war thousands of miles away against the Turks in the part of Europe that's now Hungary and got captured and made into a slave. But he must have been really hand-some or charming or both, because just like Pocahon-tas, the lady who was his master fell in love with him and finally set him free. Her name was Charatza Tragabigzanda. But I guess England's King Charles hated that name. He changed Tragabigzanda to Cape Ann because Queen Anne was his mother (I guess her silent *e* got lost crossing the Atlantic Ocean).

Professor Solescu ended by holding up my compass thingie. "So, I'm fairly certain, from the markings, this artifact came from Captain John Smith's expedi-tion here. If I'm right, it could be the oldest artifact from this area not made by Native Americans."

(I didn't know what an artifact was, so I looked it up when I got to school. It's "an object made by a human being, typically an item of cultural or histori-cal interest.")

"Is it worth money?" Georgie asked.

Granpa gave Georgie a hard look. "That's not what's import—"

Mr. Hernandes interrupted him. "It probably would be quite valuable to a collector, but then it would be shut away somewhere."

Professor Solescu took the magnifying glass away from her eye and held up our compass artifact. "If you boys would be willing to lend this artifact to Harvard, others would have a chance to view it, and scholars could examine it. Of course you'd continue to own it. We'd put a card next to it in our museum that said, 'From the private collection of Ronald Mack and Georgie Singoff.' You would actually become sort of famous."

She mispronounced Georgie's last name, but he didn't care. I could tell he was thinking about being famous.

Mr. Hernandes stroked his beard and smiled so widely I could see his teeth. "And if you wanted to sell it someday, you could."

Georgie and I looked at each other.

"It's okay with me," I said.

"Me too," Georgie said.

"Terrific," Mr. Hernandes said, leaping up from his chair. "Now we have to go to City Hall. There might be other artifacts where you found this one. We've got to get that construction halted."

Five minutes later the three grown-ups and me and Georgie were walking up the steps of the Gloucester City Hall.

"I've never been inside this building," I said as Granpa opened the door for us.

"I think we came here on a third-grade field trip," Georgie said.

He was right. Once I was inside, I remembered.

(Our City Hall is a very old building that looks really important like a church or something. There's a picture of it on my website, and you can tell me if you've ever been inside someplace special.)

"This is so cool," Georgie whispered. "The mayor is sort of like the president of the town."

Mr. Hernandes must have called ahead from his car, because we were ushered right into the mayor's office.

"Good morning, boys," the mayor said to me and Georgie after she'd greeted Mr. Hernandes and his daughter. "I'm Carla Raglan, mayor of this wonderful city. Hello, Bud."

I was amazed. Granpa hadn't even said his name. He must have seen me staring at him questioningly, because he leaned over and whispered, "I played baseball with her older brother in high school. I think she had a little crush on me back then."

"Which of you is Ronald Mack?" Mayor Raglan asked.

I raised my hand like in school . . . and then felt kind of stupid for doing it.

"And you must be George Sinkoff."

"Uh-huh," Georgie replied.

"Are you boys at RLS?" she asked.

"Um, yes," Georgie said. "I'm sixth-grade class president. Well, actually I'm co-president. Um . . . Should I call you Your Highness or Your Majesty or something?"

She smiled. "Mayor or Mrs. Raglan will do."

As we sat down in her office, I noticed there was another man in the back standing behind a video camera on a tripod. Mayor Raglan saw me craning my neck around.

"We were just taking the equipment down from last night's city council meeting," she explained. "It gets televised on the local station."

Mr. Hernandes then told Mayor Raglan why we had come and handed her the compass artifact. I guess mayors have to be really good at making fast decisions, because she barely looked at it before she stood up and grabbed her coat.

"Bring the camera, Rudy," she said to the man in the back.

Five minutes later we were all (except for Granpa . . . he had to go on a limo job) standing at the construction site. Every piece of earth-moving equipment was chugging or moving or both. There were over a dozen construction workers digging, measuring, and moving stuff. It was very noisy. Rudy videoed everything.

"Right there is where I found it!" I yelled, pointing into the trench. Every eye but Georgie's followed my gesture. Georgie was looking up at the guy controlling the excavator.

("I could totally drive that thing," he told me later.)

Then I realized Rudy was standing right behind me, aiming his camera down my arm into the trench.

"Hey, Cheesie! Whatcha doing over there?" Some kids were yelling to me from the school yard.

"So what's the deal here, Carla?" a man behind me said.

I smelled cigarette smoke (ugh!) and turned. It was the redheaded man with the big belly. He was hold-ing his clipboard and listening to the mayor, but also glancing at me and Georgie. It was pretty obvious he recognized us even though we weren't muddy like yesterday.

The redheaded man tossed his repulsive cigarette down, stepped on it, and said something to another man, who must have been the foreman, because moments later, one after another, every one of the machines shut down. The quietness was very noticeable. In fact, in a very strange way, the quietness seemed really LOUD.

"Hey, Georgie!" It was Alex Welch. He was standing in front of a whole gang of kids gathered at the edge of the construction site. If it had been only Alex—he's such a dweeb—Georgie and I would've ignored him. But lots of kids were waving and yelling, so we waved back. That's when I spotted my sister. She was standing with some other eighth-grade girls. I am very good at reading my sister's lips . . . especially when she is saying the same thing over and over: "You are in big trouble."

"Come on, boys," Mayor Raglan said. "I have just ordered a temporary halt until Professor Solescu can get some archaeologists from Harvard out here for further investigation. Let's go talk to your principal."

Georgie whispered, "Uh-oh! Are we in big trouble?"

Mayor Raglan led our group around the construction site. I guess she did not want to jump over four-foot-deep trenches. Rudy, the guy with the video camera, ran ahead. When we got to the string boundary, the waiting crowd of kids—including Goon— split apart, and we walked through with Rudy videoing us.

It was just like we were famous or something.

Chapter 8

The Time Capsule

Once inside the school building, Mayor Raglan marched us down the corridors toward Principal Stotts's office like we were in a parade. Rudy kept in front, sort of walking backward, videoing us the whole time. Because first period had just ended, the hallways were jammed with middle schoolers going to their next classes. The kids we passed were very curious.

Georgie whispered to me, "Don't pick your nose or scratch your butt. That guy Rudy is filming everything."

We turned in to another corridor, and there was Mr. Stotts. Our parade came to a halt, and the adults started talking about adult stuff. We were right next to room 113, Georgie's and my homeroom. Our door opened. Lana came out, holding a Jolly Roger hall pass.

(We're the Pirates, remember?)

When she saw me, Lana got excited and waved. But I guess she forgot that the plastic hall pass was looped around her wrist, because it flew up and hit her in the nose. I don't think it hurt, but she got suddenly embarrassed, so I looked away and pretended I didn't see what happened.

I wonder why pirates called their flag a Jolly

Roger. Who was Roger? And why was he so happy? I am going to stop writing and look it up online.

? ? ?

(Each question mark is one minute. It only took three minutes for me to find out.)

Jolly Roger probably comes from *joli rouge*, which in French means "beautiful red." In the olden days, a red flag on a sailing ship's mast meant the captain and crew would fight and fight and never offer a truce. In other words, *Don't ask for mercy! We are the meanest, nastiest pirates to ever sail the Seven Seas!*

What are the Seven Seas, you might ask? I love explorers and geography and maps, so I wrote a report for school about the Seven Seas. It's on my website. I bet you'll be surprised because the Seven Seas do not include the two biggest oceans: the Atlantic and Pacific. And it's NOT because oceans are not seas.

And why did the red flag get changed to black with a skull and crossbones? Nobody really knows.

? ? ? ?

(These question marks are because something just hit my window, and I took four minutes to

95

investigate. I think probably a bird, but there's noth-ing on the ground, so . . . back to my adventure.)

"Georgie," Mr. Stotts said, "you're going to the student government meeting this afternoon, right?"

"Uh-huh," Georgie replied.

"Fine," he continued. "I'd like you to take Cheesie as a guest and one of you give a two-minute report about what you found and why construction of the media center is being temporarily halted. And now, you two . . . back to class."

Rudy lowered his camera. "Excuse me, Mr. Stotts. May I video that meeting?"

Georgie and I were just opening the room 113 door when Mr. Stotts said, "Sure. Excellent idea."

As we walked to our seats, I whispered to Georgie, "I'm getting the feeling our artifact thingie must be really important."

"Artie-fartie thingie," Georgie whispered back . . . so I slugged him . . . which made Mrs. Wikowitz give me a stern look. I gave her a big (totally fake) smile. She did not smile back.

At lunch (pizza, which is Georgie's favorite because he is a champion slice chomper), Georgie and I sat at our normal table, which is usually all boys, but today Oddny plunked herself down right next to Georgie. Lana probably wanted to sit next to me, but I had taken a seat at the end, so there was no room, so too bad. She sat next to Oddny.

Our table is in the sixth-grader section, which is about a million tables away from where the so-called RLS "cool kids" sit. (Goon is one of those kids, so being a galaxy away is just fine with me.) But today we were the definite, total center of lunchroom attention. Tons of kids jammed our table. Everyone wanted to know about the mayor and why they were videoing and what we had found. Eight or ten kids shared treats, almost all of which Georgie ate. We were having a great lunch until someone tapped me on the shoulder . . . hard!

It was Goon, trailed, as usual, by her boyfriend, Drew. "What're you going to do when they figure out your lousy thingamajig is just a piece of junk?"

I ignored her. So did Georgie. He walked off to get another slice of pizza.

"You did trespass, you know," Goon continued loudly. "You'll probably get arrested for that."

My sister can be very convincing. I glanced at the kids around our table. Several were nodding like they sort of agreed.

"And then they'll make Mom and Dad pay for the construction delay. It'll be thousands of dollars. Maybe more!" Goon sort of puffed out her chest and looked around at everyone like she had just crushed me. "Did you ever consider *that* when you broke the law?"

I lifted my milk carton and took a long drink, staring at her the whole time. Then I wiped my mouth with the back of my hand. "Did you ever consider that a Harvard professor told us this morning what I found might be the most important archaeological discovery on Cape Ann . . . *ever*?"

That was an exaggeration, but it worked. The nodding heads stopped nodding. Two girls giggled. Goon spun around and stomped off.

Drew trotted after her, yelling at me lamely, "Loser!"

I had dissed Goon in public. My lead increased by two points. The Point Battle score was now 741–694.

Georgie returned with three slices of pizza. Kitchen lady rules are only one at a time, so Oddny gave him a questioning look.

"They love me in there," he explained with a huge grin.

"In a certain way," Glenn said, "your discovery is somewhat like unearthing a four-hundred-year-old time capsule. The artifact you found brings Captain John Smith's previously hidden past into our present."

"That is so cool," Lana said.

It *was* so cool . . . and that gave me an idea.

"Hey, guys. Since the school's putting up a new building, why don't we, the RLS students, bury a time capsule under it for kids maybe a hundred years from now to find? We could put stuff inside that would be totally interesting to kids in the future."

"Like what?" Lana asked.

"How about a pizza?" Georgie blurted, holding up a slice. "Almost everybody loves pizza. And a hundred years from now, kids'll probably be eating artificial, freeze-dried junk. You know, like food pellets. I bet they'd be really interested in pizza."

"Hundred-year-old pizza . . . eww," Oddny whined.

Everyone stared at Georgie. He shrugged, took a huge bite, and grinned, chewing loudly and open-mouthedly.

"Gross," Diana muttered.

Then Glenn spoke up.

"Actually, Georgie's idea is quite good. I wouldn't suggest including an actual pizza in the time capsule, but I believe a copy of our school's lunch menu would be very informative to children of the future."

There was a short silence while Glenn's suggestion sank in.

"And you could put a recipe for pizza along with it," Lana added, "just in case those kids wanted to make some."

"Totally!" Georgie the Pizza Mouth said. Then he swallowed, took a swig of milk, and said proudly, "Another one of my Great Ideas."

Then he burped.

After school, Georgie and I went to the student government meeting. They're in the library, last about a half hour, and take place once a week right after last period. I'm not an officer, but I always go.

I go, but I don't actually go to the meetings.

You are probably thinking, *Huh?*

Georgie's my best friend. And since he's sixth-grade co-president, he has to attend all the meetings, so I wait for him, hanging around in the computer room or doing my cross-country practice. Then we always go home together. If you have a best friend, you absolutely know why I do this.

But Mr. Stotts had invited me to attend this student government meeting, so this time I walked into the library with Georgie. Mrs. DeWitt, our librarian, waved to me from her office. She knows I write books . . . and she loves books . . . so I guess it makes sense that she is one of my favorite RLS grown-ups. I waved back.

Diana Mooney and Eddie Chapple, the other two sixth-grade co-presidents, were already there. The rest of everybody was all the other student officers plus Mr. Stotts and Mr. Amato, who is my very short, very round science teacher and also the student government faculty advisor.

Goon (eighth-grade *vice president*, but whose real title should be eighth-grade *miserable sister*) was surrounded by all four of the seventh-grade girl officers. Goon is *very* popular at RLS, which I don't understand at all because to me she is such a butter-header (remove the *ers* and you'll know what I mean).

She was jabbering about *Swan Lake*, which is a ballet, which is her favorite thing in the whole world. The girls were sooo interested in everything Goon said. One of them was concentrating so hard, a little dribble of drool was leaking out the corner of her mouth, and she didn't even know it.

How does Goon hypnotize people into thinking she is nice? I don't get it!

But I have to admit Goon is very excellent at dance and knows everything about ballet. And the music from *Swan Lake* and *The Nutcracker* (another ballet) is really good. You've probably seen *The Nutcracker* on TV. They show it every Christmas. Both ballets were written over a hundred years ago by Pyotr Ilyich Tchaikovsky. *Pyotr* is how Russians say the name Peter. Same for *Pedro* in Spanish, *Pierre* in French, *Pietro* in Italian, and *Petr* in Czech. In German, Peter is Peter. (I asked Granpa—he knows lots about languages.)

Goon saw me come into the room. She gave me a huge smile. That was weird.

I pointed to the back of the room. "Let's sit here," I said to Georgie. "My sister is up to something."

And she was.

A few seconds later, while Mr. Stotts and Mr. Amato were in the front of the room talking to eighth grader Jake Mitaro, RLS student body president, Goon, accompanied by several of her girl-ballet-drooling fans, came back to where we were sitting. She was very polite, which made me very suspicious.

"Alyssa, Hailey, Camden . . . this is my *little* brother, Ronald."

She really emphasized the word *little*.

"He's not a student officer. He's a guest. He's going to talk to us today about something *really important*."

She made the phrase "really important" sound totally bogus. Then she smiled a fake smile.

Now I was super suspicious!

"Don't be nervous, Ronald," Goon said with an even fakier smile. "The kids in here are really nice."

Huh? I never get nervous in front of people.

Goon looked at me like she felt really, really sorry for me. Then she turned to her fans. "He gets the hiccups." Then she spun around like she was in a ballet and sort of glided back to her chair. I have to admit she is very graceful. The other girls followed her like servants following a queen.

Hiccups? Why had she mentioned hiccups? I wondered.

The meeting started. Georgie leaned over and whispered, "When you tell about the thingie, you better be on high alert." He pointed at Goon. "Your enemy is planning some sort of surprise attack." You can probably tell Georgie plays lots of war video games.

Hiccups? When was the last time I had hiccups? I stared at the back of Goon's head and listened to the first discussion. It was about wearing costumes to school on Halloween, which was less than three weeks away. Decision: optional for kids, required for teachers.

Georgie whispered, "If Mrs. Wikowitz comes dressed as herself, she'll for sure win Best Witch."

I had to slap my hand over my mouth and nose to keep from snort-laughing.

Then the discussion switched to the Thanksgiving food drive for needy families. Decision: the homeroom that collects the most food gets to represent RLS in the city's annual holiday parade.

Georgie whispered, "No biggie if our room doesn't win. Now that we're pals with the mayor, we can ask to ride on her float."

I slapped my hand over his mouth to get him to shush.

Then Jake Mitaro called on Georgie.

"Cheesie's going to tell about it," Georgie said.

(If you read my last book, you know Georgie hates getting up in front of people unless he's doing his Great Georgio magic act.)

I walked to the front of the room. As I passed

Goon, she quietly went, "Hic!" And that's when I realized what her plan was. She was trying to get me to think about hiccups . . . and if I did think about hiccups, maybe I would actually get hiccups. *No way!* I thought. *I will not think about hiccups. I will not. I will not.*

"After school yesterday," I began . . . and just then the word *hiccup* went right through the middle of my brain!

Stop it! I told myself, looking out at all the kids staring back at me. Goon sat, her hands folded on her desktop, smiling her most evil smile. She quietly pretended to hiccup.

I pretended not to notice.

"After the sixth-grade basketball game," I continued, "Georgie and I trespassed—"

My chest felt weird. Kind of like way down inside, there was a bubble or something. *It is NOT a hiccup,* I told myself. *Do not even think about hiccupping.*

I took a deep breath. "We trespassed—I admit it—into that construction area. We were just goofing off, messing around, and we found—"

As I told my story, I realized I was doing three things at once:

1. I was speaking aloud, explaining how we found the Captain John Smith artifact.

2. I was thinking about hiccups even though I had told myself not to, and my mind was jumping from one question to the next.

What causes hiccups?

Something to do with your diaphragm?

What actually is a diaphragm?

How do you spell *diaphragm*?

Is there a silent *g*?

Who ever heard of a silent *g*?

Oh yeah, how about the *g* in "Silent Night"?

And then, believe it or not, the music to "Silent Night" started up in my head, and I wondered what Granpa might get me for Christmas, because he always comes up with really weird and fun gifts.

If you are a careful reader, you probably noticed I said "three things at once," but there are only two items in the list above. That's because while my mouth was speaking about Captain John Smith and my mind was zooming from hiccups to Christmas, it was like I was outside myself observing me doing both. Thinking about those two things was number three.

"Go on," Jake said, and I realized I had stopped talking and was just standing there thinking about thinking.

"Oh yeah," I said quickly. "So Georgie and I and my Granpa took this thing, this artifact, to the museum . . ."

Goon went "Hic!" It was just loud enough for me to hear.

". . . and we showed it to Professor Solescu . . . she's the daughter of the man who—"

Sometimes things happen without warning. This was one of those times.

"Hic!"

It just popped out of me. A hiccup so powerful it made me jump backward. Everyone was staring at me. I looked at Goon. Her eyes were wide and her face was all contorted like she was trying to keep from laughing.

"HIC!"

This one came out of me even louder. Everyone laughed. Goon's hee-hee was so big, she actually had to put her head down on her desk. Even Mr. Stotts and Mr. Amato were smiling. I was totally blushing.

It was in front of others and really embarrassing.

Eight points for Goon. The score was now 741–702.

I am not a quitter. I had hiccups throughout the rest of my explanation—and there were tons of giggles and snickers—but I finished telling everything. "So there will be a team (hic) of scientists from Harvard coming up to our school to dig (hic) around because maybe there are more artifacts."

"And that means," Mr. Stotts said, "construction will be temporarily halted while they do their investigation. For all we know, this school may have been built on a site of great historical importance."

"Speaking of historical importance," I said. "At (hic) lunch today, a bunch of us came up with an idea." I told Mr. Stotts and everyone else about the time capsule.

"An excellent, excellent suggestion," Mr. Amato said. His head was moving up and down so much that several kids began nodding with him.

Mr. Stotts agreed enthusiastically. "Professor Solescu thinks the construction delay will be very short. Probably no more than a week. If we can put a time capsule together before construction resumes . . ."

"Cheesie found that Artie Fact," Georgie offered loudly without raising his hand, "so I think he should decide what goes into the time capsule."

Mr. Stotts puckered his lips and sort of simultaneously nodded and shook his head. "Well, I don't think he should be the *only* one to decide. But, yes, we'll set up a Time Capsule Committee and Ronald can be the chairperson."

I looked at my sister. She was mad . . . and speechless . . . and mad.

(I put *mad* in that sentence twice because that's how angry she looked. She hates when I get anything.)

Georgie wasn't finished with his suggestions. "And since I was the only other Artie Fact finder, and we're both sixth graders, the rest of the committee should be all sixth graders. I nominate Diana and Eddie."

"That is completely unfair," Goon blurted. "What about seventh and eighth graders?"

Mr. Stotts looked directly at me. "June is right."

Goon gave me a you-lose look.

"I'm going to add the presidents of both upper

grades to the committee. And Mrs. DeWitt," Mr. Stotts said loudly to get her attention, "would you agree to be faculty advisor?"

"Of course! It'll be fun," she said from the other side of the library. "The committee can have its first meeting here at lunch tomorrow."

Mr. Stotts stood. "Sounds good. Meeting adjourned."

Georgie jumped up and shook my hand vigorously. "Congratulations! You have just become the Big Cheese!"

I grinned. Yesterday morning I was just another sixth grader at Robert Louis Stevenson Middle School. Today I am chairperson of the Time Capsule Committee.

Oh yeah.

Uh-huh.

Cooler than Goon.

Chapter 9

Harry Potter and the One-of-a-Kind Book of Uniqueness

Just before dinner, while I was playing a video game with Georgie in the living room, Granpa came up from the basement carrying bottles of his homemade root beer. "I don't share this with just anyone," he announced loudly. "But tonight is special."

Granpa makes his own root beer from a recipe he says he invented. It is really delicious, but he makes only two dozen bottles in a batch, so I don't get to drink it often.

My dad asked, "What's the occasion, Pop?"

Granpa set the bottles on the dining room table and strode into the living room. "We've got a big celebrity eating with us tonight. Just watch what I recorded off the five o'clock news."

A guest? I had no idea what he was talking about. Mom, Goon, and Dad followed him. Granpa grabbed the remote and clicked off our video game.

"Hey," I moaned. "I was winning."

"Too bad," Georgie said with a fake I'm-so-sorry face. "I would've caught up anyway."

Granpa waited until everyone was seated, then clicked the remote until a newscast he had recorded came on.

". . . migration of whales along the New England coast should continue for another couple of wee—"

He fast-forwarded until the screen switched from spouting whales and ocean shots to a woman in a museum.

"Harvard archaeologist Dr. Elizabeth Solescu announced this afternoon the discovery of—"

"That's the lady we met!" I said loudly, pointing at the TV screen. The professor was holding up the compass thingie we'd found.

"Shh!" Goon hissed.

The newscaster's voice continued, "—a four-hundred-year-old artifact from one of the earliest British explorations of Massachusetts, unearthed by two schoolboys in Gloucester."

Georgie elbowed me in the ribs. "That's us!"

"I can't hear!" Goon shouted.

The image then showed our school construction site, and there was Georgie, looking up at the excavator. I was pointing into a trench and yelling over the construction noise, "Right there's where I found it!"

The rest of the news report talked about how important our discovery was. The whole thing was only a minute long, but it ended by showing me and Georgie walking through our school with the mayor.

"You're famous, kiddo," Granpa said, ruffling his hand through my hair.

How cool was that?! Georgie and I jumped up and high-fived. Mom and Dad were smiling. Goon wasn't.

I had a bottle of Granpa's root beer at dinner. Dee-lish! Goon didn't drink any. She said she wasn't thirsty.

* * *

As Georgie and I walked to our homeroom the next morning, it seemed like the whole school was buzzing with talk about us.

Here are some of the things kids said:

1. "Can I have your autograph?" (a girl I didn't know)

2. "May I have your autograph?" (another girl I didn't know)

3. "May I *please* have *your* autograph?" (Georgie . . . being a jerk)

4. "I uploaded your newscast appearance onto YouTube. And now it's been shared all over Facebook." (Glenn . . . who showed us the video on his phone, which caused lots of kids to gather around and peer over our shoulders)

5. "You guys must think you're hot stuff." (This was Drew, Goon's so-called boyfriend. Goon walked right past us.)

Even in our classes, we were kind of like celebrities. In homeroom, Mrs. Wikowitz led a special lesson about the exploration of New England and the importance of archaeology in understanding how people lived back then. In science, Mr. Amato explained why some artifacts decay and others don't. Most articles made of iron rust (they oxidize), while things made from plants or animals get eaten up by bugs or bacteria or mold (they rot). In math, we were supposed to review converting fractions to decimals and vice versa, but Ms. Hammerbord took the first fifteen minutes of class to tell us about how she went to Montana one summer when she was in college to dig for fossils. (She found a bone from a duck-billed dinosaur, a hadrosaur, that was eighty million years old!)

At lunch, we had barely taken two bites when I looked at the wall clock and jumped up.

"Georgie! C'mon! We're late for the Time Capsule Committee meeting."

Georgie shouted, "Doin' a Dutcher!" and shoved his entire hot dog into his mouth. (If you read *Cheesie Mack Is Cool in a Duel*, you know who Dutcher was and what he could do.)

I turned to Lana. Once Oddny started sitting at our table, so did Lana. "You and Oddny come, too.

I want you to be part of the committee."

I zoomed out of the lunchroom. Georgie, his cheeks ballooned out with hot dog, was right behind, followed by the two girls. When I got to the library, the president of the seventh grade (Bobby Pinkerton) and the other presidents of the sixth grade (Diana Mooney and Eddie Chapple) were already seated. Moments later Lana, Oddny, and Georgie (he had swallowed) came in.

Mrs. DeWitt handed me the student government gavel. "You can use this to chair the meeting, but let's wait a bit. The eighth-grade president isn't here yet."

Then Goon walked in.

"Mikaela couldn't make it. But I'm vice president, so she appointed me in her place."

"She is so lying," I whispered to Georgie. "She forced her way in."

"Let's get started," Mrs. DeWitt said, but then her phone rang. "You kids go ahead," she said, heading for her office, "I'll be right back."

"Why are they here?" Goon asked, pointing to Lana and Oddny.

"I wanted to have an equal number of girls and boys," I responded. "And as head of this committee, I have that authority." I wasn't sure that was true, but it sounded good enough to shut Goon up, so I rapped the gavel on the table twice and began, "Mr. Stotts and Mrs. DeWitt said we need to make up a list of what should be in the time capsule. Lana, would you please be secretary?"

She is one of those kids who are always prepared. She took out a pencil and some paper. I rapped the gavel again. (It's fun to be chairperson!)

"So, who's got an idea?" I asked.

Over the next fifteen minutes there was a lot of discussion. Ideas came from everyone except Goon. She just texted friends and fiddled around on her phone.

Some of the ideas got rejected immediately:

1. Eddie: "My fifth-grade class photo. Then they'll know what a cool kid looked like." (Diana: "Too conceited.")

2. Bobby: "My hand-painted skateboard." (Me: "Good idea, but too big to fit inside.")

3. Georgie: "A shrunken head." (Me: "Why

ever?" Georgie: "To see if it shrinks even more!")

And some were instantly accepted:

1. Bobby: "Last year's RLS school yearbook." ("Too bad your photo isn't in it, Eddie.")

2. Oddny: "A picture of a manatee." ("Because they're funny-looking and will probably be extinct by then.")

3. Lana: "A smartphone." ("Definitely with its user's guide . . . even though it wouldn't work because the battery will be dead.")

4. Georgie and Glenn's school lunch menu/ pizza recipe idea.

5. Oddny: "A science textbook." ("They'll be so advanced, our science book will probably make them laugh.")

6. Eddie: "A one-dollar bill." ("Who knows what money will look like in the future?")

7. Me: "An official Gloucester letter from Mayor Raglan." ("It should begin, 'Dear Gloucester of the Future.'")

We were brainstorming, and it was lots of fun.

What would you have suggested? Please go to my website and tell me.

We were still going strong when Mrs. DeWitt came out of her office and opened a side door to let Mr. Stotts, two men, and a woman into the library. The woman had a microphone. The men were carrying video equipment. Goon instantly stashed her phone away.

"These folks are from cable news," Mr. Stotts announced. "They're here about the discovery. I told them about our time capsule, and they would like to video you kids in action."

"Um, what are we supposed to do?" I asked as the cable news crew began videoing.

"Just continue with your meeting," Mr. Stotts replied. "I've already contacted all your parents and gotten the okay."

"Um, any more ideas?" I asked.

No one spoke. It's weird how a camera can make people suddenly shy.

Everyone, I guess, except Goon.

"I've got an idea," she said brightly.

My sister is very clever. If there was a chance to be on cable news, she wanted to be the star.

"I would like to put a book into the time capsule. One that would be typical of what kids today like to read."

My sister is very smart. She knew exactly how a librarian would react to that kind of a suggestion. Mrs. DeWitt raised her eyebrows and nodded several times. "What an excellent idea. Do you have one in mind?"

"Yes," Goon replied, smiling at the man holding the camera. "I would like to donate my own personal copy of *Harry Potter and the Sorcerer's Stone*. Since it was the first book in the world's most popular series of children's books, don't you think it would be perfect?"

"Well, I'm just your advisor. It's not up to me. What do you all think?" Mrs. DeWitt asked.

I could tell Mrs. DeWitt *loved* Goon's suggestion. She was smiling so broadly I thought her face might split apart. (Not really . . . but in cartoons that could happen. And then her chin would fall to the floor!)

"I adore Harry Potter," Diana said.

"Super good idea," Bobby Pinkerton echoed.

I looked around the room. Every kid was nodding. The cameraman videoed them all. They looked like a bunch of bobbleheads.

"Well," Mrs. DeWitt said, "since you all agree, I think I have a way to make June's terrific idea even better. I have a special copy of that book which I think would be a much better inclusion."

"Lots of people own that book," Goon responded quickly. "What's so special about yours?"

"It's autographed by J. K. Rowling," Mrs. DeWitt explained. "It's a first edition . . . and quite valuable. If you like, I'll bring it in tomorrow."

Goon didn't say anything, but I could tell she was upset that Mrs. DeWitt had one-upped her idea. Especially since it might get on the news.

The bell rang for our next class.

"Okay. Let's wrap this up," Mr. Stotts said.

Georgie raised his hand.

"The chair recognizes sixth-grade co-president Georgie Sinkoff," I said. Since I was on camera, I thought I should sound very official.

He stood, cleared his throat, and spoke very clearly: "Mr. Chairman Cheesie, I think every kid at RLS should get a chance to be a little bit famous . . . you know, by their idea getting a chance to be in the time capsule. Therefore, I nominate that we should ask for suggestions from all the kids in our school."

It was an excellent idea. "Your nomination is approved," I said, smacking the gavel on the table. (Dad told me later I should've called for a vote.)

"I'll ask Mrs. Collins in the office to send a notice to every class," Mrs. DeWitt said.

"This meeting of the Time Capsule Committee is adjourned." I slammed the gavel down again, but this time it slipped out of my hand, flew up, and bounced off the video camera.

Nothing *broke* . . . but everyone *broke up* laughing.

Even the news crew.

And especially Goon.

You might think I would have to give Goon points,

but you can't lose in the Point Battle when you embarrass yourself.

I laughed harder than anyone.

I wouldn't even mind if it got on television.

Chapter 10

Red Cheeks

Georgie insisted I eat dinner at his house that evening. I have done that millions of times, always with just him and his dad. But this time, with everyone there for the upcoming wedding, I think he wanted someone his own age to hang with.

It was kind of fun at first. Georgie's three brothers told lots of goofy stories from when they were kids. Then Fed's girlfriend asked Ms. D about her first date with Georgie's dad.

"Was it romantic?" Ava inquired.

Georgie elbowed me, then silently and secretly pretend-puked.

"It was very special," Mr. Sinkoff said with a sly

smile. "I took her to a fancy restaurant."

"It was a burger joint," Ms. D explained.

"I was trying to make a good impression," Mr. Sinkoff continued, "but when I took the first bite of my hamburger, ketchup squirted out in two directions. One glob hit me on the cheek, and the other landed on the table in between us."

"How awful!" Ava blurted.

"Not really," Ms. D explained. "I didn't want him to be embarrassed, so I immediately stuck my finger into the ketchup on the table"—she dipped her finger into some spaghetti sauce on her plate—"and did this." She dabbed the red sauce onto her cheek.

Georgie immediately stuck a finger into the sauce on his plate and copied her. "I don't want *you* to be embarrassed!" he said.

"Me neither!" I echoed, dabbing sauce on my own cheek.

"And me!" Georgie's oldest brother, Jokie, shouted, saucing himself as well.

It was like follow-the-leader. In seconds, there were lots more sauce-smeared cheeks all around the table.

Then Marlon, who had been hiding his pregnant cat on his lap, lifted her into plain sight and dabbed her cheek.

"Now I *am* embarrassed," Georgie's dad said.

After that, things calmed down and the conversation switched to stuff about the wedding: where to put the flowers, who's in charge of music . . . you know, important for grown-ups, but maximum boring for me and Georgie.

"I'll clear the table," Georgie volunteered.

"Me too," I said.

We jumped up and carried dishes into the kitchen.

"You know what bothers me?" Georgie asked, as he dumped the knives and forks into the sink.

"What?" I responded.

"Joy is the maid of honor. Okay. I get that. But . . ."

Joy is Ms. D's daughter. She missed tonight's dinner because she's a high school volleyball and basketball star. She had a game. Her picture is in our newspaper's sports section all the time.

". . . Jokie gets to be the best man. And Fed and Marlon are ushers, but I don't get to be anything,"

Georgie said. "What's that all about?"

"I'm in charge of the guest book. You can help me," I offered.

"Big deal," Georgie muttered. "I'm the youngest. I know that. But my brothers don't even live here."

I didn't know what to say. Just then Ms. D and Mr. Sinkoff came into the kitchen with armloads of dishes.

"Ask them," I whispered, jabbing Georgie in the side (not too hard) with a serving spoon.

Sometimes you need a friend to poke you a little.

He asked.

"Of course you have a special place in the wedding," Ms. D said. "You're the ring bearer." She turned to Mr. Sinkoff. "Didn't you tell him?"

Georgie's father shrugged. "I guess I forgot." He set down his dishes and looked straight at Georgie. "I've been pretty scatterbrained about things recently. But that doesn't mean I think your role is insignificant. That ring is valuable, and it's also very important. We can't get married without it. Once you have it in your hands, everything depends on you." He patted

Georgie's shoulder. "Being ring bearer is a position of trust."

Ms. D agreed. "You'll keep the wedding ring in your pocket all through the ceremony. Then you'll . . . Oh, you know what happens then." She gave him a hug and went back to the dining room with Mr. Sinkoff.

I could tell Georgie was happy. He mumbled, "Cool," and then hummed while he put stuff into the dishwasher.

The next morning, time capsule handouts were distributed to every homeroom, and by the end of school there were dozens of suggestions from lots of kids. (Most were goofy!)

The committee met briefly in the library to pick out the best ideas, and since some of the things we selected were not available at our school, Mrs. DeWitt suggested we split the final list in half and divide into two groups of four and go around town to pick up the articles. Before I could decide who was in each group (I was really getting into being a chairperson, so I figured I had that authority), Goon stated loudly, "I'm on Georgie's team."

My sister is very sneaky. She knew I would hate being in a group with her, so that meant I couldn't be with my best friend. That's why the teams ended up: Cheesie/Lana/Bobby/Diana and Georgie/Oddny/Eddie/Goon.

"You love this. You get to be with Lana," Goon said ~~smirkishly~~, ~~smirkily~~, ~~smirkingly~~ with a smirk. I was a little bit embarrassed, so I gave Goon four points. 741–706.

Mrs. DeWitt's final instructions were, "Collect all the items and bring them to the museum before five. Mr. Hernandes has acquired a special watertight box. He'll catalog the items and pack everything up over the weekend, and on Monday, he'll give the box to the construction company. We'll have a ceremony, and then later they'll bury it secretly when they pour the foundation."

"Why secretly?" I asked.

"You wouldn't want somebody digging it up around twenty or sixty years from now and ruining the surprise, right?"

I nodded. Lana was right next to me, nodding, too.

131

Mrs. DeWitt continued, "Mr. Hernandes will also put an envelope into the museum files to be opened in exactly one hundred years. Inside the envelope will be a key to the box and a map showing precisely where the time capsule was buried."

Mrs. DeWitt was so excited she clapped her hands once. I couldn't help it . . . I did, too.

"And here's my special book, Cheesie." Mrs. De-Witt lifted her autographed Harry Potter book out of a paper bag and showed it to me. It looked brand new . . . like it had never been read. She showed me J. K. Rowling's signature, then carefully put the book back in the bag. "Do not—I repeat, do not—let this book out of your sight. It is very valuable."

"No problem, Mrs. DeWitt. I will guard it with my life!" I stashed the bag in my backpack, stood like a soldier with a super-fierce expression on my face, and then saluted.

She laughed. "I feel confident you will not let me down."

The two teams took off in opposite directions. My group went downtown. Georgie's went to the harbor. We texted progress reports to each other every few minutes. Since I wasn't with Georgie, here's his own report.

* * *

Hi! Georgie Sinkoff here again.

I can't believe Cheesie is letting me write in his book again, because of how I trashed him (HA!) last time, but anyway, here goes.

My team was:

Me = cool.

Oddny = cool.

Eddie = cool.

Goon = problem.

Most of the items on our list were a cinch to get, but our lobster thing was a giant headache. It was supposed to be something that showed how lobstering is a big deal in Gloucester.

So Eddie said, "We could take a picture of a bunch of lobster pots."

But I said, "Nah. That'll just look like a giant pile of boxes. What if we all stand in front of the pots, holding up a live lobster?"

Eddie said, "I'll do it."

Oddny said, "Me too." She then told us how, because her dad's a fish scientist, one time she was in a fish packing plant and stuck her arm up to the elbow (!) in a huge tub of fish guts.

I'd do it if you dared me!

But Goon refused to touch a lobster. I knew she's a vegetarian, so I held one up right next to her face and said, "Just hold it. No one's asking you to take a bite."

But she refused. Finally, we just took this picture.

Okay. That's what happened. And this time I didn't goof on Cheesie. (HA!)

Back to you, Cheesemeister.

* * *

On the other side of town, Team Cheesie was very efficient. Diana, Bobby, Lana, and I picked up everything on our list without any major delays. Even so, when we got to the museum, the door was locked.

Bobby pointed to the sign on the door and said, "Closed at four-thirty."

"Mrs. DeWitt said five," Diana said.

I peered in the window, but all the lights were out.

"Even librarians make mistakes sometimes, I guess,"
I said.

"What's going on?" Georgie shouted from down
the block.

I waited until everyone was together. "We'll take
all the junk we collected back to my house. I'm sure
I can get my grandfather to drive me here tomorrow

before school. Georgie and June and I can carry it all."

(I do *not* call her Goon in public.)

"Not me," Goon said, texting someone about something that was obviously way more important than the time capsule. "I've got things to do. I'm out of here."

"Where are you going?" I asked.

"None of your business, Runt." She walked away.

(Goon does not play by the same name-calling rules as I do.)

Georgie and I took all the plastic bags and envelopes with the time capsule items, said "See ya tomorrow!" to the others, and started walking toward home.

"Wait up!" Oddny shouted.

I turned around. She and Lana were whispering. Lana nodded.

"We'll walk with you a ways!" Oddny shouted. Then they ran to catch up.

I don't want you to get all weird about me and Lana. Just because I walked with her doesn't mean I like her. I mean . . . I do like her. She's smart and a fast runner and all that. But I don't *like* her. Get it?

We didn't say anything for a while. Then Oddny asked, "When they open the time capsule a hundred years from now is too far ahead to think about, but what do you think you'll be doing in . . . I don't know, pick some number of years?"

Georgie answered almost immediately. "In ten years I will be a Navy jet pilot. Or maybe Air Force."

Oddny went next. "I'm going to double Georgie. In twenty years I'll be thirty-one, so . . ." She thought for a while. "I will be a scientist like my father, and I will be married and have two kids, and I will travel all over the world studying oceans and fish."

I didn't want to go next, so I waited for Lana to go. She was quiet for almost two blocks.

Finally, "In forty years—I'm doubling Oddny— I'll be fifty-one, and I'll be living in a big city. I mean, I really like Gloucester and all that, but if I'm going to be a doctor doing research on diseases, I think I'll work at a big hospital or university or something."

The others turned to me.

"I'll double Lana. So, in eighty years I'll be ninety-one, older than my grandfather. But maybe being that old will be different then, so maybe I'll still be having adventures and still be writing books."

"Yeah," Georgie said, "the title will be *Cheesie Mack Is Getting New False Teeth*."

Everyone laughed. A few blocks farther, the girls waved goodbye, and we separated.

It's fun to think about the future. If you want to tell me what you're going to be doing in the future, I have a page on my website for that.

When Georgie and I got to my house, we went to

my room, shoved Deeb off my bed, and emptied all the time capsule items onto it.

"This is a lot of stuff," Georgie said. "I wonder if it'll all fit."

I looked at everything all spread out. "And we'll have a few more things from school . . . like the year-book."

"And some photos we have to print out." Georgie told me about Goon and the lobsters.

I laughed. Then I got an idea. "I know how to check if it'll all fit. Follow me."

With Deeb right behind, we ran down the stairs to our basement. Georgie stood watching while I rummaged around until I found a cardboard box that looked right.

"This is about the size Mrs. DeWitt told me. C'mon!"

We ran back upstairs.

Surprise!

Goon was in my room, facing away from me, lean-ing over my bed.

"What are you doing in here?" I shouted. "Get out!"

There was a flash of light. Goon turned around. Her phone was in her hand. Without a word, she pushed past me and walked out. Then I heard her door slam . . . and lock.

"What was she taking a picture of?" Georgie asked.

We examined all the stuff on my bed. Only one item looked different. Mrs. DeWitt's Harry Potter book was out of its bag, lying open to J. K. Rowling's signature.

"I don't get it," Georgie muttered.

"I do," I said, closing my door. "She's jealous. Her copy doesn't have a famous signature."

"Yeah, probably . . . ," Georgie said, grabbing the cardboard box from me. "I am very excellent at packing. I bet you anything that I can get everything into this box."

I didn't bet him. He's really good at things like that.

"Let's have dinner at my house," Georgie said as

he placed the last item in the box . . . with room to spare. "I wanna see if Squirrel has had her puppies yet."

I yelled to Granpa where I'd be and scooted out the back door. I was a few steps behind Georgie (Deeb was way ahead), but I am totally faster than he is, so I caught up to him just as we got to the won't-close gate that separates our backyards. Deeb stayed in my yard (like she's supposed to) as Georgie and I jammed through the gate at the same time, hopped over the creek without getting a bit wet, and raced across the grass to his back door. I won by two steps.

We didn't make it past the kitchen.

"Perfect," Ms. D said, sticking her arm across the doorway to keep us from leaving the kitchen. "You are just in time to try on your wedding outfits."

She pointed to two big plastic bags on hangers hung on cabinet handles. I could see black clothes and a white shirt inside the bags. From outside the kitchen we could hear music, laughter, and lots of talking.

"We're too busy right now," Georgie said. "There's a ton of homework."

That was sort of a lie. All we had was one set of math problems (fifteen minutes, max) and a short story to read for Core (another twenty minutes, max-max).

Ms. D didn't budge. "None of that baloney, mister. This'll take no time at all. Try them on."

Jokie and Charlotte came through the door past Ms. D. The music and chatter got much louder with the door open. They picked up some chips and dip and went back out. Charlotte ruffled Georgie's hair as she passed. The door closed, and the noise lessened.

"Yeah, okay," Georgie muttered. "But I'm not going to try them on here and have my brothers and their friends all goof on me. We'll change at Cheesie's. Then we'll come back and show you. But first, has Squirrel had her babies and can we go look at her?"

Ms. D smiled. "The answers are no and yes. Then come right back and let me see you in these clothes. I've got a million things to do before the wedding, and you guys are numbers one and two on my list."

Then she ruffled the hair on both our heads. (You have probably noticed adults love to do that to kids.)

The living room was packed with a crowd of brothers, wives, girlfriends, and buddies. Georgie's brothers grew up in Gloucester, but they now live in Boston, New York, and Philadelphia, so I guess when they come back here, they want to see their childhood friends. I know I would . . . if I ever moved away from Gloucester.

Marlon had taken over Georgie's room, so we figured that's where we'd find Squirrel. But she wasn't there. We prowled around the second floor, looking in closets and under beds. Finally we found her in Georgie's dad's bedroom, lying on top of his dresser.

"Hello, fat cat," Georgie said softly, stroking her from head to tail. "Look at your giant tummy."

"How many kittens do you think she'll have?" I asked.

"I guess . . ." Georgie looked up at the ceiling like he was doing some kind of calculation. "I think . . . maybe . . . thirty-seven." Then he laughed.

(I looked it up online . . . the record for most kittens in one litter is nineteen!)

So I punched his arm. It wasn't hard—I wasn't

mad or anything—that's just a way to say "Shut up."

But Georgie staggered like I had really slugged him, instantly turning into Ee-Gorg, the insane companion of the mad scientist Dr. Frank N. Cheez. (Georgie and I invented these crazy characters in third grade.)

"Ee-Gorg sorry, master. Ee-Gorg very bad." He shambled around the bedroom with his arms in front of him like a zombie.

I began petting Squirrel and spoke in my most evil Dr. Frank N. Cheez voice: "Do you like cats, my brainless friend?"

"Mmmm . . . cats. Yes, master. Ee-Gorg like cats very much," Georgie said. "Ee-Gorg eat cats."

He lurched crazily toward Squirrel with his mouth open like he was going to bite her. For a second I thought she might get spooked, but she just lay there purring.

Suddenly Georgie stopped and picked up a small black velvet box on the dresser, next to Squirrel's tail. He opened it. Inside was a gold ring.

"Excellent, Ee-Gorg," I continued in my Dr. Cheez voice. "One ring to rule them all, one ring to find them. One ring to bring them all and in the darkness bind them."

(You probably know those words come from *The Lord of the Rings,* which IMO are really great books and really great movies.)

"Yes, Ee-Gorg," I continued. "You have found the one magic ring that can grant me immense powers. Give it to me!"

I was still playing Dr. Frank N. Cheez, but Georgie wasn't in our game any longer.

"Cool it, Cheesie. This is the ring my dad's going to give Lulu. It's what I get to carry at the wedding." He closed the box and headed toward the door.

I grabbed his arm. "Why are you taking it?"

He shook himself loose and headed down the stairs. "If I'm going to wear fancy clothes and be the ring bearer, then I'm going to keep it with me and be responsible for it. C'mon!"

We zoomed back through the older brothers'

party (snatching some treats as we passed through), grabbed our plastic bags from the kitchen, and opened the back door.

"Don't get anything dirty!" Ms. D said.

"I have the ring!" Georgie shouted back to her just before the door slammed behind us.

Deeb was waiting at the won't-close gate. The three of us raced up to my bedroom and closed the door. We got the black pants on in a flash, and the shoes at the bottom of the bag seemed obvious, but I couldn't figure out the shirt.

"Look at these ruffles. I think this is for girls. And there are buttonholes on the sleeves, but no buttons. And what're these for?" I held up some jewelry gadgets.

Georgie shrugged a how-should-I-know. "These pants are weird. Look at the shiny stripe down the leg."

"And what the heck is this?" I held up a super-wide belt made of black cloth.

"Beats me," Georgie replied. "There aren't even any belt loops on the pants."

I opened my bedroom door. "Granpa!" I shouted. "Can you come here? Georgie and I need help."

Granpa came in, took a long look, chuckled, and then got us dressed. If you know what a tuxedo is, you know why we were confused. If you don't, here's what was what.

Clip-on bow tie
[easy to put on]

Ruffled shirt
[looks like
it's for girls]

Cummerbund
[it's a belt
that doesn't
even hold up
your pants]

Cufflinks
[buttons
would
be easier]

Shiny pants stripe
[like a policeman]

Super shiny shoes
[made out of
plastic?]

When we were completely dressed, Granpa stood back and grinned. "You boys look like a couple of penguins."

"I wanna see," Georgie said. He picked up the black velvet box and walked toward the bathroom.

He was admiring himself in the mirror when I came in. Just then I heard Goon open her door, so I quickly shut and locked the bathroom door. I did not want her to see us and start teasing or anything.

The two of us stood in front of the mirror.

"Wow," I said softly. "We do look like penguins. But really classy, good-looking penguins."

Georgie nodded. "Very sharp. We look like on TV when someone wins an award."

I held up an imaginary microphone. "And the winner of the Ring Bearer Award is Georgie Sinkoff."

Georgie smiled, gave a little bow, and waved a hand to his imaginary fans in the mirror.

I continued speaking into my invisible microphone. "Would you show our viewers the award-winning ring-bearer technique you intend to use at the wedding this weekend?"

"I'd be happy to, Mr. Cheesie. Please step back. I need room."

I moved out of his way. Georgie took the ring out of its box and placed it in his pants pocket. The way he moved his hands reminded me of how he does magic tricks when he's dressed up as The Great Georgio.

Georgie spoke in a very dignified manner. "When the bride asks for the ring—"

I forgot about my imaginary microphone and became myself again. "I think your dad's the one who asks. And then he puts it on her finger." I've never been to a wedding, but I've seen movies.

"Whatever," Georgie said. "When my dad asks for it, I'll pull it out like this—" He yanked his hand out of his pocket and flung it out in front of him like he was offering it to someone. Unfortunately, the ring slipped out of his fingers, flew up and bounced off the mirror, and dropped into the sink. It rolled around like a marble. . . .

We both stood there . . . just staring in shock.

And then the ring disappeared down the drain.

"Uh-oh," Georgie said softly.

Chapter 11

Sewer Rats

In a voice I could barely hear, Georgie asked, "What do we do now?"

I was speechless for a second . . . then, "We've got to get it before it goes down the sewer. C'mon!"

We zoomed out of the bathroom and down the stairs. Like always, Deeb chased after us, barking excitedly.

"Hold on!" Granpa shouted as we passed through the TV room. "Where are you birds running to in those tuxedos?"

We didn't stop. And what came out of my mouth was sort of almost the truth. "Georgie's new mom needs to see how we look."

We went out the back door but did not go to Georgie's. I cut around the side of my house.

"Where are you going?" Georgie yelled after me.

I ran through my front yard. Deeb stopped at the edge of the street. I have trained her NEVER to go past the curb . . . even if she's chasing me.

I stopped in the middle of the street, looking down at a manhole cover until Georgie caught up.

"I asked my dad once. He said all the water and stuff from our house goes through pipes and pours out into the sewer here. We've got to get down there and find the ring before it washes away forever."

Georgie looked at me in horror. "Are you serious? Do you know what goes into the sewer?"

"Of course I do. But that's where that ring's going to go eventually. Do you have a better idea?"

We stood there silently, then Georgie shook his head. "My dad said being ring bearer was a position of trust. Oh, man . . . I really blew this one."

"We're not giving up," I said. "But we can't go searching for the ring in these clothes. Let's go show Ms. D. Then we'll figure out something."

In Georgie's kitchen a minute or so later, with the noisy big brothers' party still going on elsewhere in his house, Ms. D gave us a total tuxedo inspection. "You both look very handsome," she said.

"The wedding ring I took," Georgie mumbled to her. "Did you tell Dad?"

Just then Mr. Sinkoff entered. "Tell me what?" he asked.

"We've got to get out of these clothes before we mess them up," I said hurriedly. "Let's go, Georgie."

Before Mr. Sinkoff could repeat his question, we were out the back door. By the time we put our fancy clothes back into the bags in my room, it was too dark to search through the sewer, so we had dinner, did our homework, and then just sat in my room until bedtime, doing nothing and being miserable until I turned out my bedroom light.

After a minute of in-the-dark blanket moving and pillow adjusting, Georgie spoke. "It's gone. My dad is going to be so . . ." He wasn't crying, but his voice cracked. I waited, eyes closed, for him to finish his sentence. He didn't, but it didn't matter. I knew what he was feeling. We've been friends forever.

In the morning, Georgie was still miserable.

At the top of the stairs, I told him, "Don't give up. We'll think of something. We always do. But right now we've got to act happy. Otherwise Granpa will suspect something."

We had the fakiest smiles on our faces all through breakfast. Granpa paid no attention, but Goon knew something was up. She gave us dirty looks, but we didn't crack.

"Let's get a move on," Granpa finally said, so we loaded the box of time capsule items into his car, and he drove us to the museum.

Mr. Hernandes seemed pleased with what we had brought. "Excellent . . . excellent. I'm going to look through our museum's collection and pick out something to add to what you kids have put together."

"I've got something to add," Granpa said, pulling a piece of paper out of his shirt pocket. He laid it down on Mr. Hernandes's desk with a smack of his hand.

I leaned over and looked at it closely. It was a check for ONE MILLION DOLLARS signed by Melvyn

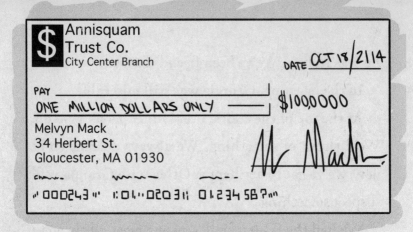

Annisquam Trust Co.
City Center Branch

DATE OCT 18/2114

PAY _____

ONE MILLION DOLLARS ONLY ——— $1,000,000

Melvyn Mack
34 Herbert St.
Gloucester, MA 01930

M. Mack

⑈ 000243 ⑈ ⑈01⑈02031⑈ 0123456 7⑈

Mack (that's Granpa's real name).

"Put that in your time capsule and you've really got something," Granpa said proudly. "I've dated the check exactly one hundred years from now and left the Pay To line blank so whoever opens the box can write a name in and collect the money."

Mr. Hernandes guffawed (which means he laughed with his mouth open wide . . . which made his huge beard flap all around).

"Do you really have a million dollars?" I asked.

"Not sayin'," Granpa responded slyly. "You want to find out, you'll have to live to be one hundred eleven and be the old man who opens the capsule." Then he gave me a squinty-evil-eye.

"Anyway, it's the thought that counts," Granpa

added, plopping down in a chair. "You kids get going to school. I'm going to argue with Bob here for a while."

We walked to school. Georgie stared at his feet the whole way. I knew why. But there was nothing we could do about the ring until we got home, so I tried to get him to think about something else. "Do you think Goon is up to something? Messing with Mrs. DeWitt's signed book. You know, taking that picture."

It didn't work. "I don't know" was all he said.

I don't remember anything about Mrs. Wikowitz's class that morning, except neither of us raised our hands or spoke. In second period, however, I got an idea. It came because Mr. Amato was talking about properties of metals. He held up a milk carton.

"This pint container has a volume of sixteen liquid ounces. If I filled it with water, the contents would weigh one pound. Sixteen ounces equals one pound. If instead I filled it with osmium, the densest, the heaviest of all metals, it would weigh more. But how much more?"

Everyone had to write down an answer. Before I tell you what I wrote, make your own guess.

Do you have one? If so, keep reading.

I like to guess at things. But I don't just guess randomly. I try to make what my mother calls an "intelligent guess." That means you think of a good reason for your guess. So here's what I thought:

1. I have held steel or iron objects lots of times. They seem much heavier than water. My guess . . . four times heavier than water. So a pint milk carton full of steel might weigh four pounds.

2. My dad once let me hold a hunk of lead. I don't remember exactly, but it seemed about twice as heavy as steel. So if my guess for steel was good, a pint of lead would weigh eight pounds.

3. If osmium is the heaviest, maybe it would weigh twice as much as lead. Two times eight is sixteen pounds.

Could a little pint container of some metal I had never heard of actually weigh sixteen pounds? That seemed ridiculously heavy, but that was my guess. Only Eddie Chapple guessed higher. When he said one thousand pounds, Mr. Amato chuckled and patted his pretty big belly. "That's even more than I weigh."

The answer was twenty-two and a half pounds!

I was closest . . . and that gave me my idea. "Mr. Amato? How about gold?" I asked. "Gold's heavy, too. Right?"

"Very heavy. Nineteen times heavier than water," he said. "That's why prospectors panned for gold in creeks. They'd scoop up material from creek bottoms with a pan and slosh it around in the flowing water. The rocks and dirt would wash away, but the nuggets and flakes of gold would be so heavy, they'd stay in the bottom of the pan."

I had to tell Georgie there was still a chance! Maybe the ring hadn't washed all the way into the main sewer.

Mr. Amato continued. "Today we use other methods to find metal. Have any of you ever used a metal detector?"

Glenn raised his hand. "I have a metal detector. I've used it to find coins and other metallic objects at the beach."

Mr. Amato then explained how metal detectors work (something to do with magnetic fields), but I was too busy thinking about finding Georgie's ring. After class I asked Glenn, and he said I could borrow his metal detector.

I got so interested in metals, I asked Mr. Amato lots more and ended up putting a page with interesting facts about them on my website. Did you know, for example, that if you make a spoon out of a metal called gallium, and stir a cup of hot tea with it, the spoon will melt?

I was late meeting up with Georgie in the lunchroom because Mr. Stotts stopped me in the hall.

"We're going to bury the time capsule on Monday, and, weather permitting, the whole school will assemble outside for a short ceremony. How would you like to give a little speech?"

"Um, okay," I responded. "But what do I say?"

"Something about the past, the future. Make it

short, very short. Mayor Raglan's going to be there. But the main thing is the TV coverage. The cable news guys want you on camera again. I don't know, Cheesie. I guess you're famous now." Mr. Stotts smiled and ruffled my hair.

Georgie was already sitting at our table when I arrived with my tray. Normally he'd be eating seconds by now, but he was still so miserable, his food was almost untouched, and he was sort of slouched. As I told him what I had learned about gold in Mr. Amato's class, he straightened up, and when I said we could use Glenn's metal detector, he sat up and took a big bite of his burrito.

Georgie wanted to go metal detecting immediately after school, but we both had practice: cross-country for me, basketball for him. And anyway, Glenn runs XC with me, so we couldn't have gotten his detector early. (In case you didn't read my last book, "XC" is the abbrev for *cross-country* . . . and in case you didn't figure it out, "abbrev" is my abbreviation for *abbreviation*.)

Georgie and I live only a few blocks from Glenn,

but even in only that short distance, we used his metal detector on lawns and in a small park and found two nickels, two pull tabs from soda cans, a motorcycle license plate, and a rusted screwdriver with a broken handle.

"This is going to work," I assured Georgie as we climbed the stairs to my bedroom toting our backpacks and the metal detector. Knowing Goon might be listening, I whispered, "If the ring's there, we'll find it for sure."

As we passed Goon's room, I glanced in. She was sitting on her bed, holding a book. But not like she was reading. More like she was inspecting it. I held up my hand . . . and like two soldiers on patrol, Georgie and I halted. For a long moment, Goon didn't notice us spying on her. Then she did, jumped up, and closed her door.

"Very suspicious," I said quietly, dropping my backpack onto my bed. "Did you see what she was looking at?"

"Uh-uh. Nope. Did not," Georgie replied. "Let's get outside."

"Well, I did. She was looking at her Harry Potter book."

"So?" Georgie was in a hurry. He dumped his backpack next to mine, picked up Glenn's metal detector, and was out my door.

I trotted after him, grabbed two flashlights from our laundry room cabinet, and caught up with him at my front door. "Goon read that book years ago. It's been sitting untouched on her shelf forever. But since we got Mrs. DeWitt's autographed copy, she's been all of a sudden very interested in it again. I don't get it."

Georgie shrugged "Who cares," then walked quickly into the street and over to the manhole.

I live on a very un-busy street. It's a dead end, so the only cars that drive on it belong to the people who live here. Some grown-ups might not allow it, but my parents have let me play ball in our street since I was seven.

Georgie switched on the metal detector and waved it over the manhole cover. It beeped like crazy!

I gave him a look. "Duh! The whole thing is made out of metal."

Georgie switched it off. "We've got to get this open," he said, poking at the manhole cover with his shoe.

I looked at the cover. It had one metal word in raised letters on it: SEWER. It was perfectly round except for one notch. "See this?" I said, bending down and sticking my finger in the notch. "I bet you pry it up from here."

I tried lifting. No way.

"We'll need a crowbar or something," I said.

"Forget it," Georgie said. "Even if we get it open, right out here in broad daylight some-one will see us and call the cops or the sewer police or whatever."

What happened next was weird. Deeb was at the edge of my yard, excitedly jumping around because she knows she is not allowed in the street. The weird thing was she was barking. Deeb is not a barker, and anyway, there was nothing to bark at. Georgie and I walked to the curb. When we got close, Deeb took off, running toward the backyard.

"What is up with your dog?" Georgie asked.

"No idea," I said, trotting after her. "Let's get something to open that manhole. Even if we might get caught, we've got to try."

I was planning to go in my back door and then down to the basement to look through Granpa's tools, but when I got to the backyard, Deeb was standing by the won't-close gate, barking her head off.

"Something's up," I muttered to myself.

You probably won't believe what I'm going to tell you next, and actually, I don't know what to believe myself, but when I opened the gate, Deeb, who NEVER leaves my yard without an order from me, just zoomed out, splashing through the creek. About ten yards downstream, she stopped, turned around, and barked. It sounded like (I'm not kidding!) "Rurri Yupf! Rurri Yupf!"

Which I think is Dog Language for "hurry up."

Georgie pushed by me, carrying Glenn's metal detector. "I know what she wants!" he shouted. "She's telling us we can get into the sewer from our clubhouse! Let's go!" He ran after Deeb. I followed.

We don't actually have a clubhouse. In fact, we don't even have a club. A little ways downstream, the creek goes under a road, and there's a four-foot-wide metal pipe that comes out of the concrete wall that holds up the road. When Georgie and I want a secret hideout, we climb inside that pipe. That's our so-called clubhouse.

Sure enough, Deeb was waiting below the pipe.

"Good dog!" I said, rubbing her head. I lifted her into the pipe, and she sniffed her way to the back. About six feet in, there's a steel screen that blocks you from going any farther.

"I take back everything I ever said about your smelly dog," Georgie said. "She's a genius. You wait with Deeb. I'm going to get tools to open that screen."

Georgie ran back downstream. I climbed into the pipe and picked up the notebook Georgie and I always leave in there. (In it Georgie draws cartoons, and I write good ideas, jokes, and all about things Georgie and I do.) I flipped on my flashlight, pulled the pencil out of the spiral binding, turned to a blank page, and began drawing a diagram of where the road above my head went. Then I drew my street where I thought it was. If our clubhouse pipe was part of the sewer system, it had to connect (if I'd drawn the streets, the creek, and the pipe in the right places . . .) right there! I drew an X. We had just finished reading *Treasure Island* in Core. "X marks the spot," I said to Deeb. Then I turned off my flashlight and waited.

It didn't take Georgie long. He had wrenches, pliers, a hammer, and a couple of tools I didn't know the names of. He tossed them clankingly into the pipe and climbed in after them.

I turned on the flashlight and showed him my map. "Pirate treasure. Gold doubloons. Finding a gold ring. Pretty much the same thing," I said.

"Yep," Georgie said. He picked up a wrench and hooked it onto one of the bolts that held the screen in place.

Georgie is very strong. I could not have loosened a single bolt. But he undid four. One of them was so stuck, he had to hit the wrench with the hammer! Then we bent back the screen.

"I'm leaving Glenn's gadget here," Georgie said. "All these pipes are going to be metal. We'll have to find the ring the old-fashioned way . . . with our eye-balls."

He pulled back the screen, and I squeezed through. Then I braced my back against the wall of the pipe and used my legs to push the opening wide enough for Georgie to squeeze through after me. I looked back at Deeb. She was lying down in the pipe. I guess she figured she had done her job and now could rest. We shined our flashlights into the darkness. Only ten feet ahead, the pipe met another similar pipe in a T. We could see no farther.

"If my map is right," I said softly (when you are inside a pipe, there is no need to speak any louder), "my house is that way." I pointed to the left.

In all the times we sat in our clubhouse, there was never any water coming through the screen, so when we turned left into the second pipe, we were surprised to get our knees wet. I pointed my flashlight down. There was a shallow stream that didn't seem to be moving. It didn't smell, but the bottom of the pipe did feel a little slimy.

"This is kind of gross," I muttered.

Georgie aimed his flashlight down the pipe. It lit up the sides, but straight ahead was total darkness. We could not see the end.

"Do you think there are really alligators in sewers?" I asked.

Georgie gave me a don't-be-a-dope look. "Of course not. What would they eat?"

"Kids who crawl through pipes," I replied with a laugh.

Neither of us had moved. Our feet were still at the T.

"Did you hear something?" Georgie whispered.

I shook my head. *If I were a goblin, this would be my dream house,* I said to myself. I leaned backward and looked out. Deeb hadn't moved. The light was dimming. It would soon be dinnertime.

"I just thought of something," Georgie said. "If we go in, how will we find our way out?"

"My map?" I suggested.

"It'd be better if we had a long ball of string," Georgie said.

"Like Tom Sawyer," I said.

Ms. Higgins had read *The Adventures of Tom*

Sawyer by Mark Twain to us last year in fifth grade. It's a really famous book, and in it, Tom and his friend Becky Thatcher follow a ball of string they'd unrolled to find their way back out of a cave. "I have a roll of kite string in my roo—" I stopped because Georgie suddenly grabbed my arm.

"Look!" he blurted in a scared whisper.

His flashlight was pointed into the long, dark tunnel. The last time I'd stared into the pipe, I had seen nothing but bare walls and unending blackness. Now, at the edge of that darkness, three sets of reddish eyes stared back at us.

Underground Quest
(Rated "D" for Disgusting)

LIVES REMAINING: 2

All but one of Makko's clan were now gone. Only minutes earlier, Makko had watched Old Gramps get overrun and eaten by three of the largest slime mice he had ever seen. Only Zinkov remained alive. Sure, Zinkov was the biggest, cleverest sorcerer Makko had ever quested with, but with just two of them left, could they get through this dark maze alive?

"You tell me, Zinkov . . . why do they call 'em mice?" Makko whispered. "Big as tigers, those are."

Zinkov didn't answer. He moved his light blaster slowly from side to side, peering into the darkness.

Makko knew slime mice. They attack . . . and then attack again. He was ready.

"Did you hear something?" Zinkov whispered.

Makko spun around.

Too late . . .

(Screen turns dark red, then goes black.)

* * *

LIVES REMAINING: 1

Zinkov and Makko were the only ones left.

"I've cast the string spell," Zinkov whispered. "We go in . . . it'll get us back out."

He started to crawl forward, but Makko held up his hand. Zinkov halted.

"Did you hear something?" Zinkov whispered.

Makko spun around.

Too late . . .

(Screen turns dark red, then goes black.)

* * *

LIVES REMAINING: 0

Makko knew slime mice. They attack . . . and then attack again. He was ready.

"Did you hear something?" Zinkov whispered.

Makko spun around, expecting slime mice, but this was worse. Much worse. A stench globbin reached out for him. Makko flicked his small osmium wand, and its last fireball shot out, striking the stench

globbin in the neck. The repulsive globbin collapsed. In his dead and stinking hand was the gold ring they'd been seeking.

"Dumb luck," Makko said to Zinkov. "Now let's get out of here."

(You got the ring! Congratulations. Game over.)

* * *

After I finished writing the last chapter, I took a break and went over to Georgie's to play a video game with him. When I ran out of lives, I came back home and started thinking about what a video game would be like if it took place in disgusting sewers and other underground places. So I wrote what you just read. You can probably figure out where I got my ideas. If you can't, there's a page on my website that explains everything.

Kids have asked me, so yes . . . I like writing *and* I like playing video games, but there's a difference between those two activities. When you finish writing, you have something. When you finish a video game, the screen goes dark.

Think about it.

Chapter 12

Switcheroo Times Two

"It wouldn't have worked anyway," Georgie grumbled.

We had returned his father's tools and were climbing the stairs at my house.

"Too dark. Too wet," I agreed. "And too many creatures."

I stopped suddenly at the top of the stairs. Georgie bumped into me.

"What?" he asked.

From inside the closed bathroom, we could hear Goon singing loudly.

"She's taking a bath . . . and look." I pointed at her bedroom door. Goon had shut it, but one of her slippers had stopped it from closing all the way. "Wait here," I said, tiptoeing across the hall.

"What are you doing?" Georgie whispered a bit too loudly.

Wait, I mouthed silently.

I pushed Goon's door open and moved quickly toward her bookshelf. I'd been thinking about this a long time, and now was my chance. I heard footsteps and turned around. Georgie was at the door, his head poking in.

"What are you doing?" he repeated, tiptoeing in.

I didn't answer. I scanned the books, found the one I was looking for (you guessed it . . . *Harry Potter and the Sorcerer's Stone*), and pulled it off the shelf. Georgie came up behind me as I opened to the first page.

"Just as I thought," I whispered, jabbing my finger at the writing. "Goon switched books. This one's signed by J. K. Rowling. It's Mrs. DeWitt's."

I quickly rearranged some of her other books so the gap where the Harry Potter had been wouldn't be noticeable and zipped out of her room, pushing Georgie ahead of me. Goon was still singing.

Once the two of us were back in my room with the door closed, I dropped the book onto my bed and paced around the room. "What a sneaky plan! Once the time capsule gets buried, Goon gets to keep the really valuable book."

Georgie rolled Deeb out of his way and sat on my bed. "And none of us—not even Mr. Hernandes—opened the other book to see there's no signature in it. Wow! No one would've noticed for a hundred years." He picked up the book and looked at the signature. "But remember when she was in your room? Why did she take a picture?"

"Dunno. Doesn't matter," I said.

Boy, was I wrong! It mattered big-time, but I didn't find that out until much later.

Georgie closed the book. "She's pretty clever."

I stopped my pacing. "Uh-huh. Pretty clever . . . but not clever enough. Tomorrow you and I'll go to the museum and switch the books back."

"Why not just rat on her to your folks?" Georgie asked. "It'd serve her right."

"Yeah . . . but nah. Mrs. DeWitt made me promise never to let her book out of my sight. I've got to do this secretly. If I tell on Goon . . ."

"I get it," Georgie said.

"And c'mon! Think of how totally hacked off Goon will be after the time capsule is buried and she discovers she has her own book back." I am sure I had a most devilish grin on my face.

Just then we heard Goon come out of the bathroom. Georgie and I looked at each other for a moment and then burst into hysterical laughter.

In the morning, Georgie's head was still on the pillow when he announced, "I've got a Great Idea. We'll buy another ring to replace the one I lost. After breakfast get your bike and meet me in front of your house with as much money as you can scrape up." Then he left to go have breakfast with his brothers.

Buy another ring? I wasn't sure if that really was one of Georgie's Great Ideas, but it was worth a try. So here's what I did:

1. I emptied my piggy bank. (Even if you think piggy banks are for little kids, don't

laugh. Lots of nights I talk my dad into giving me his pocket change, so there was over eleven dollars in it.)

2. I stashed the book I had taken from Goon's room in my small backpack (not my school one . . . it's too big) and took it down to breakfast.

3. I gobbled some cold cereal and borrowed five dollars from Granpa ("I need to buy a wedding present" . . . not really a lie).

4. I ran outside to where Dad was just getting into his limo (he had to drive some tourists around Cape Ann) and borrowed another five dollars ("I need to buy a wedding present" . . . not really a lie, again).

Then I went out front, straddled my bike, and listened to a mockingbird while I waited for Georgie.

Mockingbirds are called that because they mock (copy) the calls of other birds. (I am going to write a report on them for science, and if Mr. Noa, my music teacher, lets me use it in his class, it'll be kind of like using one bird to "kill two birds with one stone."

Either way, my report will be on my website if you want to read it.)

"How much did you get?" Georgie asked me when he arrived.

"A little over twenty-one dollars," I said as we pedaled toward town.

"I had eight bucks, and I got ten more from Jokie. Everyone else was still asleep," Georgie said. "Almost forty bucks. That's got to be way more than enough to buy one stupid little gold ring."

"Your troubles are almost over!" I replied.

Boy, was I wrong!

When we told the lady in the jewelry store what we wanted, she just shook her head. There must have been two dozen wedding rings in the tray she showed us, but the cheapest one cost almost three hundred dollars! Georgie was stunned. His mouth hung open.

"How much is the most expensive one?" I asked.

The lady was very nice. Even though she had another customer waiting, she showed us one that cost over *two thousand dollars*! And it was just gold . . . no diamonds or rubies or anything.

(Did you know diamonds are made of 100 percent carbon? Mr. Amato told me if you put a diamond in oxygen and burned it, it would turn completely to carbon dioxide gas with absolutely nothing left over. Wouldn't that be a waste?)

"What do we do now?" I asked when we were back outside on our bikes.

"I'm cooked." Georgie sighed. "I guess I just go home and tell my dad what a jerk I am."

"We need to stop by the museum," I said.

Georgie didn't respond.

Normally I would've tapped my knuckles against his skull and said, "Hello? Anyone in there?" but he was too miserable. So I just said, "The time capsule? The book Goon stole . . . remember?"

Georgie nodded, and we started pedaling uphill past lots of downtown stores.

"Hi, Georgie. Hi, Cheesie." It was Joy Dinnington, Ms. D's daughter. She was just coming out of a shoe store with another girl, one of her high school friends, I guessed. After the wedding tomorrow, Joy would be Georgie's stepsister. I'd seen her a few times with Ms. D and watched her play basketball, but I didn't know her very well. Starting tomorrow, however, she'd be my neighbor.

"Hi," Georgie said to Joy with absolutely no joy in his voice.

"Wow. What's wrong?" she asked.

Joy is sixteen, blond, kind of pretty, I guess, and taller than her mom. Normally I wouldn't have noticed, but because of the mission we'd been on, I definitely spotted the three gold rings on her fingers and her dangly gold earrings. After what the lady in the jewelry store had taught us about how expensive gold was, I *knew* none of those things could be real.

Georgie started to reply, but I cut in. "Those are really cool earrings. And really neat rings. We—I mean Georgie—wants to buy something like that for somebody. You probably know where to get them."

Joy gave Georgie a big smile. "Do you have a girlfriend, Georgie?"

The girl with Joy giggled.

I looked at Georgie, hoping he would realize I had a plan hatching in my head.

"Um, kinda," Georgie mumbled.

I shouldn't have worried. That's the thing about best friends. Sometimes you don't have to communicate at all. Sometimes you just know what the other person is thinking.

Joy told us where to go. A little while later we were in a store that sold all kinds of girl stuff like bracelets, necklaces, and . . . rings. Lots of rings. And not one of them cost more than forty dollars! In less than five minutes we found a gold ring (but not real gold) that looked *exactly* like the one Georgie had lost. Even with tax, we had money left over. We stopped in a donut shop to celebrate!

Then we rode to the museum.

Mr. Hernandes was on the phone, but he put his hand over the mouthpiece and whispered, "What do you need, boys?"

"We've got one more item for the time capsule," I said. I took the book out of my backpack and showed it to him.

He nodded and whispered, "You'll find the box in there." He pointed into the room where I had first seen his professor daughter looking at all the Native American arrowheads.

Georgie and I went into the other room. The box, made of some kind of shiny metal, was on the table. (Mr. Hernandes told me later it was stainless steel, the same material they make refrigerators and dishwashers out of. That meant it wouldn't rust or rot during the hundred years it would be in the ground.) It wasn't locked, so I lifted the lid, spotted the other Harry Potter book, and swapped them, quickly stashing the one I took out in my backpack. Then I closed the box.

Moments later Mr. Hernandes came in, holding a clipboard. "That's strange. I already had that book on my list as being checked in."

He walked past us and opened the box. Georgie and I looked at each other but didn't say anything. He picked up the book I had just put in, opened it to the page where the signature was, then nodded once and put everything back the way it was.

"Strange," he muttered, looking at the list on his clipboard carefully. "I don't usually make mistakes like that." Then he turned around and said, with a big smile stretching his beard sideways, "Well, no matter. I will see you boys Monday morning."

He reached out to pat us on our backs. But since I was wearing my backpack, and it had Goon's book inside, I sort of spun out of his reach and stuck out my hand.

"It's been a pleasure to work on this with you, Mr. Hernandes."

We shook. Then Georgie and I left the museum.

"Something's weird," I said as we walked to our bikes. "He checked the signature. Did you see that?"

"Yeah. So?"

"That means he probably looked before, too," I continued.

I was onto something, but before I could figure out what was bothering me, Georgie yelled, "Race you home!"

I should've stopped right then and looked at the book in my backpack, but I didn't. Georgie had challenged me, so I stood up on my pedals and pumped hard.

Georgie was five bike lengths ahead, but I am much faster than he is, so I began gaining on him. But after a few blocks I started thinking about how the messes we'd been in were just about cleaned up, and how that was way more important than if I beat him. So I pedaled just hard enough to stay the same distance behind all the way home.

"I win!" Georgie shouted as we pulled up in front of my house.

We were both out of breath.

"Georgie," I panted. "This has been an excellent day. I think our problems are almost over."

Boy, was I wrong!

Chapter—

Triskaidekaphobia*

Just as I was starting this thirteenth chapter, Granpa looked over my shoulder and said, "Most hotels don't have a thirteenth floor because lots of people think thirteen's an unlucky number."

I'm not superstitious, but what could it hurt to be like those hotels and leave this chapter out?

If you are superstitious, please go to my website and tell me how.

* Triskaidekaphobia (tris-kai-deck-uh-FOH-bee-uh) means fear of the number thirteen.

Chapter 14

Second-Story Sneaker

I had the Harry Potter book in my backpack. My next problem was how to get it back onto Goon's bookshelf.

Once we got to my house, Georgie and I raced upstairs. As usual, Goon's door was shut, but we could hear her talking to someone on her phone.

We went into my room. "Like last time," I said softly, "we just wait for Goon to go to the bathroom." I looked at my shelf of games. "How about Yahtzee?"

We sat on my bed, playing Yahtzee with my door wide open so I could keep an eye on Goon's room. An hour later we got bored, so we began what turned out to be a super-long game of Monopoly. Georgie and I each went to the bathroom once. Goon never left her room.

"Your sister must have a bladder the size of a basketball," Georgie muttered.

"That's it, Georgie!" I said, jumping up from the bed and knocking over three of Georgie's Monopoly hotels. "I know what to do. Watch Goon's door. I'll be right back."

I raced down to the kitchen, got milk from the fridge, frozen strawberries and mango chunks and vanilla ice cream from the freezer, and whipped up a blender full of fruit smoothies. I took a sip . . . DEE-LISH! I'd made a little mess, but when I gave a small glassful to Mom, she said she'd clean up. I poured the rest into a couple of huge glasses, stuck two straws in one and one in the other, and walked back upstairs. (It is way too risky to run with full glasses of deliciousness.)

I handed Georgie the glass with two straws. "Don't drink it all. I'll be right back."

Then I knocked on Goon's door. I could hear her inside, still chattering on her phone. She didn't respond, so I yelled, "I made strawberry-mango smoothies for Mom and me and Georgie . . . and I had some left over! If you want it, open your door."

A moment later her door opened, and she stuck out a hand while continuing her phone conversation. ". . . a picture of me and Drew at the park. What? No way! Gary is absolutely not cuter than Drew! Barf!" She took the glass without even looking at me and closed her door.

I was lucky Goon hadn't taken longer to open her door. Georgie had already sucked down half our smoothie.

"No matter how big her bladder is," I said, pulling our supposed-to-be-shared glass away from Georgie the Hog, "it won't be long now." I took a big drink through my straw.

Sure enough, about ten minutes later (I had passed Go twice and Georgie had just landed on my Marvin Gardens hotel!), Goon came out of her room (still on her phone) and went into the bathroom.

"Now!" I said, grabbing the book from my backpack and scooting across the hall.

NO! Her door was locked. I slumped back to my room and plopped onto the bed so hard I messed up the entire Monopoly board. I was winning, but I didn't care. I sat there for a moment, then got up, walked over to my window, and looked out into my backyard. Because it was a warmish day, my window was open a few inches. I could smell autumn. It's a leafy sort of smell.

"It looks like we're out of ideas," I muttered.

Sometimes ideas just pop into my head without my doing anything.

Goon poked her head out the bathroom door and yelled, "Hey, Mom! Could you bring me some shampoo? We're out, and I want to wash my hair."

I spun around. "Georgie! I've got a plan. Follow me!" I shoved the book into my backpack, put it on, and ran down the stairs. Georgie was right behind. We passed Mom coming up the stairs with the shampoo.

"Where are you going?" she asked me.

"It's such a nice day . . . we're playing outside. Bye."

Once we were in my backyard, Georgie asked, "What's the plan?"

I pointed up to Goon's bedroom window. Just like I figured, on this warm day it was partially open like mine was. "Let's get your dad's ladder. I'm going in!"

Two minutes later, Georgie and I came out of his garage carrying an aluminum extension ladder. Those are the kind that you slide one part of to make them longer. We toted it through the won't-close gate and into my yard.

"We have to be really quiet," I said as we leaned it up against the back of my house. "No banging against the walls."

Georgie pulled on the rope that extends the ladder until it reached Goon's window.

"You hold it steady while I go up," I said. I looked around to see if anyone was watching, then climbed up to the second floor. I am absolutely not scared of heights. I have climbed trees taller than the top of my house.

Hooked onto the side of Goon's window was a giant circular spiderweb. In the middle was a fat spider that had just caught a fat fly. She (I'm just guessing it was female) was wrapping spider silk around her prey, spinning it around and around with her legs. I felt sorry for the fly.

"What are you looking at?" Georgie whispered.

"Cool spider," I replied, pointing at it.

"What are you boys doing?" It was Ms. D, calling from Georgie's back door.

"Looking at a cool spider!" Georgie yelled back.

"For a science report," I whispered down to Georgie. (It wasn't exactly a lie. Maybe I will do a report on spiders.)

"For a science report!" Georgie yelled to Ms. D.

"Research, huh? Good job. But be careful." She went back into the house.

Goon's window was open a few inches, so I lifted the screen away from the window (to be honest, I think I sort of broke something getting it off) and motioned for Georgie. He scampered up the ladder and took the screen from me. I raised the window and pulled myself into her room. I had just taken the book out of my backpack and slid it onto her shelf *exactly*

where I had taken the other one from when the door started to unlock! I motioned frantically for Georgie to put the window back the way it was. Then I dashed into Goon's closet and pulled the door shut.

It was dark. I heard Goon's footsteps. My heart was pounding so hard I could feel it. And I was thinking so hard I could almost hear my own thoughts. *What if Goon needs some clothes? What if she stays in her room until dinner?*

I stood there in the dark listening to her moving around. Then her hair dryer came on. I was trapped. A few minutes later it went off. Goon began singing to herself. Then her cell rang.

"Hi," she said. "Sure. I finished drying my hair. Uh-huh. Come over now."

Oh, great! I thought. *In a few minutes one of her friends will be here, and I'll be trapped for hours. I really wish I hadn't drunk such a big smoothie.*

"Okay," Goon said, "But hurry up. You can help me do my fingernails. I don't know. Sort of pinkish, purplish. Or maybe greenish, bluish. Hold on, Jasmine's calling on the other line."

Call her! That's it! Silently I dug my phone out of my backpack and dialed my home. The house phone started ringing.

Granpa answered, "Hello."

"Granpa," I whispered very softly, "would you ask Junie—"

"Hello!" Granpa repeated. "I can't hear you."

"Granpa?" I whispered. "Would you ask Junie—"

"Can't hear you. Call back." Then he hung up.

I redialed. It rang once.

"Hello!" Granpa said loudly.

"Granpa," I whispered a teeny bit louder. "Would you ask June to come to the phone?"

"June!" Granpa bellowed from downstairs. "Telephone!"

I heard June open her bedroom door. "Who is it?" she yelled.

"Cheesie needs to talk to you!"

"I'm busy!"

I whispered into my phone, "It's very important."

"He says it's very important!"

"Tell him to call my cell!" she screeched angrily.

"I can't. Granpa, please get her on the phone."

"Junie!" Granpa yelled even louder. "Come get this phone! I am not your personal answering machine."

"I'll call you right back," Goon said to whichever friend she'd been talking to.

I waited a few seconds until I was sure she'd gone downstairs, then shot out of her closet. Good old Georgie! The window was back the way it had been and her screen was up. I zipped out her door and into my room. Georgie was waiting, slurping the last of our smoothie.

Moments later Goon stomped up the stairs. "Idiot!" she shouted at my closed door, then slammed hers.

I high-fived Georgie.

Mission accomplished.

Chapter 15

Ring Around the Georgie

I was pretty proud of myself. I thought Georgie would be totally happy, too, but after the excitement of our second-story sneaking wore off, he got kind of quiet.

"What's the matter?" I asked.

"I don't know. I've been looking at this ring we bought." He had placed the fake ring in the real ring's black velvet box. "I mean, it looks okay. But do you think I'm really going to get away with this?"

"Maybe," I replied. What I really meant was no.

"You're right," Georgie said.

When you have a best friend, mostly they know what you really mean.

"I'm going to tell my mom the truth," he said, popping up to his feet.

He didn't say "Lulu." That was the first time I ever heard him call her Mom.

I put my arm on his shoulder. "Do you want me to come with you?"

Of course I knew the answer. He nodded.

~~Ms. D~~ Georgie's mom was in the kitchen with Joy, Charlotte (Jokie's wife), and Ava (Fed's gf). Someone had just baked cookies, and the smell was terrific.

Georgie's mom smiled when we came in. "Would you boys like some hot cocoa or milk and some cookies?"

"Uh-huh," Georgie replied in a soft voice, "but could I talk to you privately first?"

Her smile disappeared. "Of course." She put down her coffee, got up from the table, and opened the door to the dining room.

"Cheesie too," Georgie mumbled, motioning me to follow.

The three of us went through the dining room into the empty living room.

"Where're my dad and my brothers?" Georgie asked.

"Upstairs, trying on their fancy duds," Georgie's mom said with a small smile. "I'm hoping they'll look as handsome as you two boys did."

She sat on the couch and motioned for Georgie to join her. I sat on a big soft chair.

"What's up, Georgie?" she asked.

Normally I don't notice anything about what people are wearing (light blue dress with a dark blue apron that had blotches of flour from the cookies on it), so why this time? Maybe because I was really paying attention? I don't know.

Georgie took a deep breath. "You said I could be the ring bearer. And then Dad told me he trusted me to do it right. So I took the ring." Georgie opened the black velvet box and held it out to her. A shaft of sunlight slanting in through the window made the fake ring shine brightly.

"Your wedding ring . . . ," Georgie started to explain, but his voice got caught in his throat. He swallowed. "This isn't it. I lost the real one. It went down the sewer. So Cheesie and I bought you a new one."

His mom took the fake ring out of the box.

"Please don't tell Dad," Georgie pleaded.

She slipped the ring onto her finger and held her hand up in front of her. "It's beautiful, Georgie."

"You're not mad?" Georgie asked.

"Not at all." She took the ring off and put it back in the black velvet box. She looked at me, then back at Georgie. "Do you think there's any chance we could find the other ring . . . maybe get it out of the sewer?"

I shook my head. So did Georgie.

"We tried," I said. "We really did."

She gave Georgie a hug and handed him the black velvet box. "This ring will be perfect. And we don't have to tell your father. It'll be our little secret. At least until after the wedding."

We went back into the kitchen and ate cookies . . . a lot of cookies!

Chapter 16

Everything Goes Wrong!

For any normal adventure, this is exactly where the story would begin to finish up. Here's what would happen:

1. There'd be a happy wedding where Georgie, the happy ring bearer, would hand over the fake ring, and his happy father and happy new mom would live happily ever after.

2. The next day Georgie and I would participate in the time capsule ceremony at our school, and we'd be on TV with Mayor Raglan and be kind of famous.

3. And then, sometime after that, Goon would find out how I messed up her sneaky steal-the-

book plan, and I'd get to laugh at her for the next one hundred years!

But this was a Cheesie adventure, so you can bet nothing was normal.

"Hey, Cheeseman, why the big grin?" my dad asked at dinner that night.

Georgie wasn't at the table with my family. He'd gone out to a fancy night-before-the-wedding restaurant with his dad and mom and everyone else in his house.

"I'm just excited about Monday," I said. I wasn't going to volunteer anything about the lost ring or the book swap.

"Oh, the time capsule," Dad said.

"Tell everybody what the most valuable item in that capsule is," Granpa said, poking me with his elbow and giving me a squinty-evil-eye.

Of course I knew what Granpa was hinting at. But I was feeling so happy and relaxed, I decided to have some fun with my answer. "There are two very valuable items in the time capsule," I said. "And both of them involve this family."

Mom had a forkful of food halfway to her mouth. "I'm very intrigued," she said.

I was in such a good mood that I began speaking like I was a TV newscaster. "The item with the highest money value was contributed by Mr. Melvyn Mack of Gloucester, Massachusetts. Mr. Mack, a well-known and generous supporter of museums and archaeology, has donated one million dollars."

Granpa stood and took a bow. "I wrote a personal check," he bragged.

"Good plan, Pop," Dad said. "No one will know how broke you are for a hundred years."

"And the second item of great value," I announced, "was suggested by Miss June Mack, vice president of the RLS eighth grade. This lovely young woman is a talented dancer and a dedicated, hardworking, co-operative, trustworthy, delightful member of the RLS Time Capsule Committee."

Goon knew I was making fun of her. She gave me a dirty look, but I ignored her and kept talking.

"However, since Miss Mack's copy of the extraor-dinarily famous book was unsigned and therefore totally ordinary, the Time Capsule Committee included Mrs. DeWitt's autographed copy instead."

"You're wrong," Goon objected. "My book is signed."

"No, it isn't," I countered, smiling a little.

"Is too," Goon continued. "I'll prove it."

She jumped up from the table and ran upstairs. My smile turned into a huge grin. This was perfect. It would be an excellent Point Battle victory. In a few seconds Goon would let out a hideous shriek when she opened the book and found *no signature*!

I waited.

No shriek.

And I waited.

No shriek.

And then I heard her coming down the stairs. She still wasn't shrieking. In fact, she was humming. And when she danced into the dining room holding the Harry Potter book, she spun around once like a ballerina and gracefully dropped into her chair.

She was smiling.

I wasn't.

Goon opened the book and turned it so everyone could see J. K. Rowling's signature.

I was stunned.

"It's signed . . . see?" She held it right up to my face.

I was super stunned.

"It might not be signed by J. K. Rowling," she said with a big smirk, "but it's signed."

"What do you mean, honey?" Mom asked.

"Well, I knew I'd never get J. K. Rowling to sign my book, so I took a photo of the signature in Mrs. DeWitt's, and I copied it. I even used the same color pen."

I was super-duper stunned.

"Interesting," Dad said.

Goon set the book down on the table. "Maybe it's not her real signature, but it makes me happy."

I was so stunned I wasn't sure I was breathing.

Granpa took a long look. "Darn good work, Junie. Not that I know what K. J. Growling's signature looks like, but this one looks authentic to me. You may have a career as a counterfeiter in front of you."

Mom looked sternly at Granpa. "Don't even tease about that, Bud." Then she turned to Goon. "You cannot tell anyone your book is authentic. If you do, you'll be guilty of forgery."

Goon pretended to be shocked. "Mom! I would never do that. I know it's not authentic."

But it *was* authentic! By switching books, I had stupidly made sure of it. And because of me, the book with Goon's fake signature was sitting in a stainless steel box in the museum!

"May I be excused?" I said, and then sort of choked and had to take a sip of water.

"No dessert?" Mom asked.

I shook my head and ran up to my room. Then I texted Georgie: Call me ASAP.

I waited. He didn't call, and I was miserable for the next three hours. Finally Georgie walked into my bedroom. He was in a great mood.

"Excellent restaurant. I had four desserts. Actually only two of my own and then most of Ava's and

Charlotte's. But they didn't eat—"

I put my hand over his mouth and asked, "Why didn't you call me?"

"Mmmf," he replied.

I took my hand away.

"Mom said I should turn my phone off," he said.

So I told him everything.

He did not look too concerned. "Why don't you do what I did about the ring and confess to your mom? She'd get the book back from your sister."

I shook my head. "If I did that, Goon would laugh at me for the next hundred years." (And I would lose big in the Point Battle.)

"We need some kind of commando plan to switch the books again," Georgie said. "Where's she now?"

"Back in her room."

Georgie thought about that for a moment, then started to get undressed. "There's nothing we can do about it tonight. But when I get up tomorrow morning, I will have a Great Idea."

Georgie was asleep in minutes. It took me a lot longer.

Chapter 17

Sink Off*

When I got up, Goon and her stupid book were all I could think of. Georgie was still asleep, so I ran into my backyard to see if Goon's window was open. Maybe we could do the ladder thing again. But nope. Closed. When I came back inside, Mom looked up from reading the Sunday paper.

"What's with wearing pj's outside?" she asked.

"I don't know, Mom. I was, um, looking at a spider." (I actually was . . . sort of. The fat spider was still in her web by Goon's window.)

"Curiosity is a valuable trait," Mom said, "but it's pretty cold out there for pajamas."

I must have looked upset or anxious or something

* Georgie here: Isn't this the greatest chapter title you've ever seen?!

else mothers are good at spotting, because she laid her paper down, reached out, pulled me close, and whispered, "Here's a question for an eleven-year-old. How old will you be when you decide you're too old for hugs from your dear old mother?"

I leaned backward and stared up at the ceiling like I was working on a really hard math problem. "How old? Hmmm. Let's see. Maybe . . ." I paused, then dived in and gave her a huge hug.

"NEVER!" I shouted.

Maybe you'll think what I did next was sort of babyish, but I promised to tell the truth about my adventures, so here goes.

I stayed in that big hug for a long time. At first it was a squeeze-hard kind of hug. Then we both relaxed, and I just sort of snuggled onto Mom's lap. I closed my eyes, and it felt like I was four or five. And I sort of forgot about Goon and her stupid book.

"Cheesie!" Georgie yelled from upstairs. "I have a Great Idea!"

I jumped out of Mom's arms and started for the stairs.

"Ronnie, darling," Mom said, "do me a favor, please. June left this here on the table last night. Please take it up to her."

Peeking out from under the Sunday paper was the Harry Potter book!

"Thanks, Mom!" I hugged her one more time and grabbed the book.

"Georgie!" I yelled, sprinting up the stairs two at a time.

He was waiting at the top.

"We've got to get dressed and get over to the museum right away," I whispered. I was holding the book behind my back.

"I think maybe it's closed on Sunday," he replied.

"Then we'll have to call Mr. Hernandes or someone. Look!" I held the book up high. "My sister left this downstairs."

And then, faster than I could react to, Goon whooshed out of her room and snatched the book out of my hand.

"Oh, thanks," she said.

Before I could say or do anything, she spun around,

went back into her room, and locked the door. Goon would make a great spy. I didn't even see her coming.

It didn't exactly fit with the Point Battle rules, but causing me to go from my-problems-are-over to back-in-the-same-mess was worth something. I gave Goon a point. My lead was shrinking: 741–707.

I trudged into my bedroom. Georgie followed and closed my door. I plopped down in my desk chair.

"I can't believe it," I muttered. "I had it. Now we're back where we started."

"Okay. Never mind. It doesn't matter." Georgie stared right at me. "I told you I'd come up with a Great Idea . . . and here it is."

He took a deep breath.

"First," Georgie said, "I go back to my house and get my giant squirt gun."

"I hate this idea so far," I said.

"Then we fill it with water. It would be cooler if we mixed ink into the water, but I don't want to get too crazy."

"I'm not listening," I muttered.

"Then you march over to your sister's bedroom

door with my water cannon while I hide in here."

That got me a little interested.

"You pound on her door until she opens up. And when she does . . ."

I sat up straighter. This was sounding better.

". . . you blast her! Then you run downstairs and she chases you and I run into her room and grab the book. I bring it back here, and we're done! Simple as pie. How's that?"

I had to admit it was an almost Great Idea.

Almost Great.

But not Great enough.

"There are two problems," I said. "First, it's Sunday. My parents are home. I will definitely get a major punishment."

Georgie shrugged.

"Maybe the punishment would be worth it," I continued, "but the second problem is everyone's been talking about that book for the past day, so as soon as dripping-wet Goon got back to her room, she'd definitely notice that it was missing."

I could tell that Georgie hadn't thought of those

problems. He stuck out his lower lip like he was pouting.

I patted his head. "Almost Great, Georgie."

We spent the next several hours hanging out in my room trying to think up another way to get the book back.

None, nope, and nothing.

Mom suggested twice we go outside to play. "The wedding's at three. It's now or never."

But we had no interest. We stayed upstairs with my door open to keep an eye on Goon. We even ate lunch in my room. Then Granpa stuck his head in.

"You guys want to see a dead whale? One of my buddies at the fire department said there's a big one washed up at the beach."

Book or no book, you definitely cannot pass up an awpic (*awesome* + *epic*) opportunity like that. In no time, we had jackets and hats on and were in Granpa's car.

"I hope it really smells really bad," Georgie said as Granpa parked in the beach lot.

The sky was gray and a cold wind was blowing, so

there were only a few other people as curious as we were.

"It's a fin whale," Granpa said.

It was huge! The biggest creature I had ever seen.

Georgie ran right up to the dead cetacean (seh-TAY-shin), which is what whales, porpoises, and dolphins are, and stepped off its length.

"Fifty feet long!" he shouted. "And very smelly!"

There was some driftwood lying nearby, so I picked up a long branch and handed my phone to Granpa. "Take my picture, okay? I want to pretend I harpooned it."

After Granpa snapped the photo, I took my phone back from him and began taking pictures and recording voice notes about the whale. You know, things like size (I remeasured, and Georgie was accurate), color (dark gray with a whitish area under its chin), how many little crabs were feasting on it (more than ten), and whether it had baleen or teeth (baleen).

"Granpa, lend me your Swiss Army knife. I want to chop off a piece of blubber."

He was standing upwind so he wouldn't have to

smell it. "No stinking blubber in my car," he said, shaking his head.

"Please! Mr. Amato really likes when students do independent investigation, and tomorrow I'll tell the whole class what I saw."

I really like whales. Maybe I'll be a cetologist (whale scientist) when I grow up.

Granpa finally agreed. "Okay. But I'll do the cutting. I don't want you hacking your nose off."

He knelt in the sand next to the whale and made the first cut. The skin was really tough and slippery. He had just gotten the blade in when his phone rang.

"Answer it, Cheesie," Granpa said, pointing to his jacket pocket. "I don't want whale goo on my phone."

It was Mom. "Come home now! Right away! Immediately! Chop-chop! It's time to get ready for the wedding."

That was the end of our whaling expedition. Granpa hurried us into his car. It would've been so cool to have a hunk of smelly blubber for show-and-tell.

Darn.

(What's the coolest thing you've ever brought to show-and-tell? Please go to my website and share it.)

When we got home, Georgie and I ran to his house to get our fancy clothes. Everyone was zooming around getting ready. We grabbed our tuxedo bags and were heading back to my house when Mr. Sinkoff yelled from his bedroom, "Has anyone seen the wedding ring?! It was on my dresser."

"I've got it!" Georgie shouted back.

Mr. Sinkoff came trotting down the stairs. He was wearing striped tuxedo pants just like ours and buttoning his ruffled white shirt.

"Where is it?" he asked. Mr. Sinkoff seemed very anxious. I guess it was because he hadn't been married in a long time.

"Um, I showed it to Mom," Georgie said. "It's over at Cheesie's." He was a little nervous, but I don't think Mr. Sinkoff noticed, because he was *more* nervous.

"Okay. All right. That's fine," Mr. Sinkoff said. "Do not—I repeat, do not—forget it."

Georgie started to give his dad a thumbs-up sign, then stopped in midair. "Did you hear that?"

"What?" I hadn't heard anything.

Mr. Sinkoff said, "I heard something, too."

Georgie got very still. So did I. We were standing in the kitchen, holding our tuxedo bags over our shoulders.

Then I heard a tiny sound: mew.

"Uh-oh," Mr. Sinkoff said softly. "Marlon!" he yelled . . . and walked out of the kitchen. "Where's your cat?"

We followed him.

Marlon appeared at the top of the stairs. "What's going on?"

"Why now?" Mr. Sinkoff said to himself. Then louder, "Marlon, get down here! I think it's time."

Marlon came bounding down the stairs. He had the bottom half of his tuxedo on as well. Mr. Sinkoff put his finger to his lips, and we all stood absolutely still.

mew

Marlon reacted instantly. "Squirrel's down here somewhere. Georgie, you and Cheesie check the laundry room. Dad and I'll look in the front of the house."

Georgie flung his tuxedo bag over a kitchen chair and ran straight into the laundry room. I plopped my bag on top of Georgie's and followed. My first thought was to look behind the washer or dryer. But Georgie pointed at the door that led to their basement. It was open about four inches.

"I bet I left it open when I put my dad's tools back."

mew

The sound was a teeny bit louder. It came from down the steps.

"Marlon!" Georgie yelled. "She's in the basement!"

Marlon was at our side in seconds. Mr. Sinkoff stood behind us, holding his head in his hands and muttering to himself, "She has to do it right now?"

Georgie and I followed Marlon into the basement.

"Well," Marlon said proudly, "I guess I'm an honorary father. Look at these cute puppies." He was standing next to a beat-up easy chair. Squirrel was on it, licking one of her four kittens.

Georgie reached out to pet one of them, but Marlon pulled his arm back. "Let Squirrel make her mother connection with her babies. You don't want to get your human smell on things. It might confuse them."

We oohed and aahed until Mr. Sinkoff shouted down the stairs, "Enough with the cats! Are any of you planning to be ready for my wedding?"

That was our signal to move into super-speed mode. Georgie and I zipped up the stairs, grabbed our clothes bags, and were out the back door and across our yards in record time. Deeb got excited when we ran past her, and followed us up the stairs.

"Did either of you touch that dead whale?" Mom asked from her bedroom doorway. She was wearing a fancy dress and putting on earrings.

We both shook our heads, but she obviously didn't believe us.

"Get in the bathroom and wash all the way up to your elbows before you even think of putting your tuxedos on."

We dropped our clothes bags on my bed and ran into the bathroom. Granpa was already in there, half his face shaved, the other half still lathered up. Georgie and I squeezed in on either side of him.

Granpa growled, "Watch your elbows and arms here, boys. One wrong move and I might slit my throat . . . or yours." He turned on a trickle of water and rinsed his razor blade under it.

"Mom says we've got to wash the whale juice off," I said, twisting the faucet to pour out more water.

Granpa shaved. We washed.

"What the blue blazes is wrong with this sink?" Granpa bellowed. Water had risen to the very top. He turned off the faucet and fiddled with the drain lever. The water didn't go down.

"June washed her hair. I bet she clogged it," I volunteered.

"There's got to be a better way to run this house," Granpa grumbled. He wiped the last of the shaving cream off his face and strode out of the bathroom. Georgie quickly shut the door. He had a very strange look on his face.

"Cheesie, listen to me. Cheesie! Oh my gosh," he whispered excitedly. "I promised I'd come up with a Great Idea, right?"

"You mean squirting Goon?" I asked. "That

wasn't Great. That was *Almost* Great."

Georgie had a wild gleam in his eyes. "What if . . . Oh my gosh, what if it isn't Goon's hair?" He pointed at the water in the sink. It still hadn't drained. "What if it's . . . what if it's the ring?"

There was a short silence. And then both of us screamed. Then we instantly got very quiet.

"Stay here," I said. "I'll be right back."

I zipped across the hall to my room, grabbed Glenn's metal detector, and was back in the bathroom in eight seconds. It was a new world's record.

I switched the detector on and shoved it into the cabinet under the sink. As soon as it neared the plastic drainpipe, it began to beep. And when we touched it to the place where the pipe curved, the beep turned into a screech!

"Cheesie! Oh my gosh! Cheesie! Oh my gosh!" Georgie said over and over.

I have never done any plumbing in my life, but I knew sort of exactly what I had to do.

"I'm getting some tools. Don't let anybody in," I said.

I ran out, heard Georgie lock the door behind me, and was down two flights of stairs and in the basement in a flash. I grabbed all the tools I thought I'd need and headed back up. Since everyone was upstairs getting dressed, I didn't have to worry about being seen until I neared the second floor. That's when I got low, moved slow, and peeked. Then ran to the bathroom door and knocked.

"Go away, June!" Georgie said. "I'm doing things in here."

"It's me," I whispered loudly.

He opened the door and let me in, then closed and locked it again.

"Your sister banged on the door twice while you were gone," Georgie explained.

I dumped the tools on the floor with a loud clatter.

"What's going on in there?" Mom shouted from her bathroom (which is on the other side of the wall).

"Just cleaning up!" I shouted back.

I had no idea where to start. (I bet most kids wouldn't know, either.) This book is not exactly supposed to be a lesson in plumbing repair, so all I'm going to say is when we took lots of things apart, water squirted up to the ceiling until we found the knobs under the sink to turn it off.

"Try undoing this pipe," Georgie said, pointing to the curvy plastic pipe.

I found a wrench that seemed to fit and turned. It wasn't easy with Georgie's head in my way. It didn't budge.

"Let me do it," Georgie said. He gave the wrench a big yank, and the plastic pipe came apart. When it did, all the water in the sink rushed out onto the two of us and all over the floor.

Sitting in the middle of the puddle were two things: a huge clot of Goon's hair . . . and the gold ring!

Chapter 18

The Imaginary Water Cannon

"Get out of the bathroom," Goon screeched from the hallway. "You've been in there forever. If I'm late for the wedding, I will kill you so bad you'll wish you were dead!"

"Leave me alone!" I yelled back. "I am having a serious bathroom problem!"

It was kind of true. I was having trouble putting the sink back together. No matter how I did it, there were a couple of parts left over.

"Move it, boys! Thirty minutes!" Mom yelled through the wall.

"That's good enough," Georgie said. "We better get dressed."

We used two towels to mop up the water on the floor and wrapped the tools in them. When we opened the door, Goon was standing right outside. She was completely dressed.

"Your makeup looks weird," I said.

I have no idea what makeup is supposed to look like, but I knew saying *anything* about it would aggravate her and make it less likely she'd notice our towel bundles. And she didn't. She just pushed by us into the bathroom. I glanced over my shoulder.

Bonus!

She had left her bedroom door ajar. Now was my chance to swoop into her room again and recapture the book.

She was reexamining her makeup with the bathroom door open. Bummer! If I dashed by, she'd see me.

"Now would be a perfect time for your squirt gun Great Idea," I muttered to Georgie.

Remember how Georgie sometimes dresses up as The Great Georgio and does magic tricks? Well, what happened next was as magical as anything he had ever done.

1. Georgie turned toward the open bathroom door, holding his arms up like he was holding a squirt-gunny water cannon.

2. He aimed his imaginary blaster at Goon.

3. He pulled an imaginary trigger at the exact moment Goon turned on the sink faucet.

4. My amateur plumbing job exploded and water shot out, splashing Goon right in the face!

Goon let out a huge squeal! Dad and Granpa came running.

Noise! Water! Chaos!

I do not remember thinking about what I did next. I just did it. I sprinted into Goon's room, grabbed the book, and ran back to my room. I hid it under my pillow just as Granpa, on his knees, turned the little knobs under the sink. That shut off the water, but the noise continued. Goon was wailing. Her dress was wet. Her hair was ruined. She stomped back to her room and slammed the door.

For the next several minutes I was given a major verbal spanking by: first Dad, then Granpa, then Mom. When I explained why we had taken the sink apart and when Georgie showed the ring, Dad quieted down and Granpa seemed a little impressed.

"You two know less than nothing about plumbing," he said, "but I give you aces for the way you—"

"No!" Mom interrupted. "No aces for anybody! You two may have ruined June's day." Mom was steaming. "Georgie, your mother will learn about this. And Ronald, you will be punished."

Then she went into June's room to console her, fix her hair, and help her find a new outfit.

The wedding went off as scheduled. And I have

to admit Georgie and I looked extremely cool in our tuxedos. And we both did our jobs very excellently. I got everybody to sign the guest book. And when it was time for the ring, Georgie acted very serious as he pulled it out of his pocket and handed it to his dad

(not flinging it like last time!). I know Ms. D was expecting the fake ring, so when Mr. Sinkoff slipped the real gold one (much heavier, remember?) onto her finger, she was surprised. She couldn't help herself. Right in the middle of the ceremony, she turned to Georgie, held up her finger, and said, "What's this?"

Georgie grinned, gave a gigantic fist pump, and whooped, "Solid gold!"

With all the excitement, Goon never noticed the book was missing from her shelf.

Chapter 19

Cable News Cameras

I took Mrs. DeWitt's book to school on Monday. Before class started, Lana and Oddny came running up to me and Georgie.

"Mrs. Collins in the office said the cable news people are coming this afternoon, and you two will be on national TV," Lana said. "I'm so excited for you!" Then she totally embarrassed me right in the school corridor in front of everyone by giving me a hug.

At lunch, Georgie asked, "How are you going to get the book into the time capsule?"

I had no idea.

Georgie leaned across the lunch table and whispered, "You could just keep it, you know. Nobody would find out for a hundred years."

I shook my head. "Goon would see it was missing from her shelf. And anyway, if I did that, I'd be just what I thought Goon was . . . a thief. And what if we're alive then because people are all living longer? I do not want to be an old guy known as Cheesie the Book Crook."

Immediately after school, all the students gathered out on the field in front of the construction site. The custodian had set up a sort of stage. On it was the stainless steel time capsule, a microphone stand, and chairs for the very cool, important people: Mr. Stotts, Mayor Raglan, Mr. Hernandes, Georgie, and me.

We were all sitting and ready to go, and kids were waving to us from the crowd, but everything had to wait until the cable news guys turned on their cameras and gave a signal that it was okay to start.

"Look," Georgie said, pointing to the side of the crowd. My mom, dad, and grandfather . . . and Georgie's mom and dad were standing there. His mom was waving.

Mr. Stotts went first. "Our school sits on a very

important part of this continent. Some of the early explorers . . ."

I can't remember the rest of what he said, because I was thinking hard how to get Mrs. DeWitt's book, which was in my backpack under my chair, into the time capsule.

Then Mayor Raglan gave her talk. "Gloucester, the oldest seaport in the United States . . ."

I can't remember the rest of what she said, either. Same reason.

Then came Mr. Hernandes. "Why do we have museums? It's because they preserve and exhibit artifacts like these two boys found right over there."

I can't remember the rest of what he said, because Georgie and I were next, and I was thinking about what I was going to say.

Mr. Hernandes was just finishing up his short talk when I noticed the cable news reporter lady holding a cell phone to her ear and making signals to her crew. Suddenly the video cameras went off. The lady with the cell phone walked up to Mr. Stotts and said something I couldn't hear. Mr. Hernandes stopped talking, and we all watched the crew rapidly moving equipment into their van.

In less than two minutes, the entire cable news team had packed up and driven away. I had no idea why, and I didn't find out until evening.

Then it was my turn to speak.

Georgie and I walked to the microphone. He lowered it to my height, and then stood next to me while I told everyone how we found the Captain John Smith compass thingie. All the time I was talking, Goon stood right in the front of the crowd of kids, pretending to hiccup. She was trying to get me to embarrass myself again, but it didn't work! I decided to embarrass her back. But with my parents watching, this was going to be very tricky.

"Mr. Hernandes," I said, "would you please unlock the time capsule? I have one more item to go in it. Georgie, would you get me my backpack?"

Mr. Hernandes was surprised, but he got up from his chair and unlocked the box while Georgie pulled my backpack out from under my chair and brought it to me.

I cleared my throat. "Being chairperson of the Time Capsule Committee is a position of trust. And Mrs. DeWitt entrusted me to care for her very valuable book. She made me promise never to let it out of my sight. So that's what I did." I pulled the book out of my backpack. "Here it is."

I lifted the lid of the time capsule and took out Goon's book. I held both of them high in the air.

"Mrs. DeWitt's book is signed by J. K. Rowling. It's authentic." I waved the book in my left hand, then lowered it and waved the other. "This other book is a fake. It has a fake signature. It was never signed by J. K. Rowling. It was fake-ily signed by my sister. This fake book was what has been in the time capsule."

Goon's face turned red. She looked both angry and embarrassed. I looked at my mother. She looked angry, too. Now came the tricky part.

"So I thank my sister, June Mack, vice president of the RLS eighth grade, and member of the Time Capsule Committee, for the use of her duplicate book. It enabled me to keep my promise to Mrs. DeWitt. With my sister's help, I sort of never let this book"—I lifted up my left hand—"out of my sight."

Kids on both sides of Goon congratulated her with pats on the back. Her angry face disappeared. I looked at my mother. She was applauding.

Victory.

I had embarrassed Goon and un-embarrassed her. I decided to give myself no points. The score was still 741–707.

Chapter 20

Smelliness Rules!

After dinner that evening Granpa shouted, "Hey, boys, that whale we saw is on the news!"

Georgie and I ran into the TV room. The lady reporter who had been at our school was talking.

". . . because this immense fin whale carcass, which washed up on a Gloucester beach yesterday, has begun to decompose, creating a dreadful smell and a potential health hazard, local officials have authorized a cleanup squad to cut it into pieces, cart it away, and bury it."

On screen, a bunch of workers in protective clothing were working on the dead whale with chain saws. A Cat backhoe loader was lifting hunks of whale into a truck. The big fat redheaded guy from our construction site was operating it.

"Now you know where your camera crew went," Granpa said. "When it comes to choosing between you and a stinking pile of whale blubber, I guess you're not exactly famous."

Chapter 21

Hello, Kitty!

So that's the end of my fourth adventure. Afterward, here's what happened:

1. Georgie's brothers left. He now has a mom and a big sister in his house.

2. Mom gave me a huge punishment for my bad plumbing. I was grounded until Halloween, and I had to do all my sister's chores. It cost me sixteen points. The Point Battle score was 741–723. It was a huge loss for me, but I'm still ahead, so totally worth it.

3. Granpa took Georgie and me to the Harvard Museum, where we saw our compass thingie in a glass case. Just like Professor

Solescu promised, our
names are on the wall
next to it. So maybe,
in a sort of way, we
are kind of exactly
famous.

4.   Marlon is going to give one of the kittens
to Georgie as soon as it is old enough to leave
Squirrel. It's a boy. Georgie named it Captain
John Smith. Georgie says he is going to train it
to climb trees and catch sewer rats.

As you probably know, you can tell me whether
or not you liked this adventure by going to my website. If you want to, please do it right away because I
didn't even finish writing this story before another
adventure began, so this will be the last chapter of
this book because I have to start on my fifth book
right away before I forget everything that happened.

Whew!

I'm not going to give away what happened in my
fifth adventure, except I will tell you that it has a lot
to do with Halloween.

If you have read all four of my books, you've gone through about nine hundred pages. That's a lot of reading.

Whew!

And it's almost 160,000 words. That's a lot of writing.

Whew!

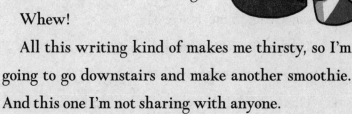

All this writing kind of makes me thirsty, so I'm going to go downstairs and make another smoothie. And this one I'm not sharing with anyone.

Except you! Take a sip. . . .

Then go to my website and tell me if you liked my smoothie . . . or this book . . . or whatever.

Signed:

Ronald "Cheesie" Mack

Ronald "Cheesie" Mack (age 11 years and 4 months)

CheesieMack.com

(Even though this is . . .) **The End**

(. . . there's more on the next page about my website.)

Lots of Website Links

1. Rules for the Point Battle. (page 3)
2. If you do or don't like this book or just want to say something to me. (page 3)
3. Granpa reciting the alphabet forward and backward without the vowels. (page 8)
4. Glenn explaining the speeds of light and sound and how to tell the temperature using crickets. (page 10)
5. Favorite cheers. (page 22)
6. Caterpillar earth-moving machines. (page 40)
7. Do you like sushi? (page 52)
8. Explaining my mom's tricky questioning. (page 72)
9. Gloucester City Hall and famous buildings you've been in. (page 87)
10. What are the Seven Seas? (page 95)

Acknowledgments

I greatly appreciate all the librarians and media specialists who invited me into their schools and libraries. I could not write in an eleven-year-old voice without those periodic immersions in full-contact kid-speak. And, as ever, thanks indeed to editor Jim Thomas and agent Dan Lazar for their handholding and excellent advice.

YEARLING HUMOR!

Looking for more funny books to read?
Check these out!

- ❑ *Bad Girls* by Jacqueline Wilson
- ❑ Calvin Coconut: *Trouble Magnet* by Graham Salisbury
- ❑ *Don't Make Me Smile* by Barbara Park
- ❑ *Fern Verdant and the Silver Rose* by Diana Leszczynski
- ❑ *Funny Frank* by Dick King-Smith
- ❑ *Gooney Bird Greene* by Lois Lowry
- ❑ *How Tía Lola Came to ~~Visit~~ Stay* by Julia Alvarez
- ❑ *How to Save Your Tail* by Mary Hanson
- ❑ *I Was a Third Grade Science Project* by Mary Jane Auch

- ❑ *Jelly Belly* by Robert Kimmel Smith
- ❑ *Lawn Boy* by Gary Paulsen
- ❑ *Nim's Island* by Wendy Orr
- ❑ *Out of Patience* by Brian Meehl
- ❑ Shredderman: *Secret Identity* by Wendelin Van Draanen
- ❑ *Toad Rage* by Morris Gleitzman
- ❑ *A Traitor Among the Boys* by Phyllis Reynolds Naylor

Visit **www.randomhouse.com/kids** for additional reading suggestions in fantasy, adventure, mystery, and nonfiction!